In My Quest for Personal Growth, the Rest of Me Grew, Too!

(Previously published as *Happy Mother's Day. . . "Wake Me When It's Over!"*)

Toni Sorenson Brown

St. Martin's Paperbacks

NOTE: If you purchased this book without a cover you should be aware that this book is stolen property. It was reported as "unsold and destroyed" to the publisher, and neither the author nor the publisher has received any payment for this "stripped book."

In My Quest for Personal Growth, the Rest of Me Grew, Too! was previously published under the title *Happy Mother's Day. . ."Wake Me When It's Over!"*.

IN MY QUEST FOR PERSONAL GROWTH, THE REST OF ME GREW, TOO!

Copyright © 1996, 2000 by Toni Sorenson Brown.

Excerpt from *Validate Me Quick; I'm Double-Parked!* copyright © 1995, 1999 by Toni Sorenson Brown. Excerpt from *Check the Lost and Found, My Mind is Missing* copyright © 1996, 2000 by Toni Sorenson Brown.

All rights reserved. No part of this book may be used or reproduced in any manner whatsoever without written permission except in the case of brief quotations embodied in critical articles or reviews. For information address St. Martin's Press, 175 Fifth Avenue, New York, N.Y. 10010.

Library of Congress Catalog Card Number: 96-68196

ISBN: 0-312-97078-1

Printed in the United States of America

Token Ink edition / March 1996
St. Martin's Paperbacks edition / April 2000

10 9 8 7 6 5 4 3 2 1

Words of praise for Toni Sorenson Brown and the Shirley You Can Do It! books

"The SHIRLEY YOU CAN DO IT! books offer a realistic, warm-hearted approach to everyday living, with a twist of humor that is uniquely Toni Brown. I love a book that has me laughing and crying . . . all on the same page. Toni's books will move you to that, page after page." —Marie Osmond

"It is a small treasure with a large impact. It can be read in one evening and savored for many nights to come . . . VALIDATE ME QUICK is like finding a new friend that understands how the daily frustrations of life can sometimes become overwhelming." —*Davis County Clipper* (Utah)

"Witty and captivating . . . Recommended to all those weary moms and wives who feel they are lacking appreciation."
—*Horizon News* (Salt Lake City, Utah)

"Until now, there has never been a series of books written especially for women by a woman. The idea is a singular one in a saturated market . . . As the readers get to know Shirley, they will discover that they know a little bit more about themselves. Her powerful, humorous messages have a universal appeal to all women." —*Park City's E.A.R.* (Utah)

"The well-placed humor and reaffirming quality of the work make it appealing . . . an entertaining book about self-discovery and the female experience . . . the perfect gift for any woman."
—*Salt Lake Observer*

The Shirley You Can Do It! Books from Toni Sorenson Brown and St. Martin's Paperbacks

Validate Me Quick; I'm Double-Parked!

In My Quest for Personal Growth, the Rest of Me Grew, Too!

Check the Lost and Found, My Mind is Missing (coming in October)

**For
Every woman who does the best she can to
mother those she loves**

Love, to be real, must cost—it must hurt—it must empty us of self.

Mother Teresa
In the Heart of the World

In My Quest for Personal Growth, the Rest of Me Grew, Too!

One

Shirley stepped onto the scale in her OB-GYN's office, carefully rocking from the balls of her tired, swollen feet to her cracked and calloused heels. Somehow she thought shifting her weight would lower the terrifying number that kept registering.

"What are we weighing in at today?" the nurse asked. *The 110-pound, never-been-pregnant nurse.*

Shirley was concentrating on keeping her balance, not to mention her bladder, under control. "*We*," she replied with more sarcasm than intended, "think *your* scale is off."

The nurse grinned good-naturedly and then looked around at the six other pregnant women who were all staring blankly at Shirley.

Shirley wasn't about to be intimidated by them, and she couldn't help thinking, *We'd make a great poster for Save the Whales*. She almost said it aloud, but instead stepped off the scale and mumbled a number.

"What did you say?" the nurse asked.

"I said this week's grand total is . . ." Shirley cleared her throat and whispered that terrifying number.

The nurse furrowed her brow and looked disbelievingly at Shirley. "Um. Are you sure? Maybe our scale *is* off."

When the agony and humiliation of the doctor's appointment was finally over, Shirley took solace in the fact that only three weeks remained until her due date. She refused to allow for the probability that she could go "over" her due date. Never mind the fact that her three previous children had all come at least one week late. That would not happen this time.

This pregnancy was so different from her first one. Shirley was now the mother of a teenager. Wasn't there some biological rule against that? Maybe her body had betrayed her, but if so, she was grateful for the double cross. This baby was a blessing. If only it would just arrive before she faced every wife's nightmare of weighing more than her husband.

Three weeks.

Twenty-one days.

If this baby did not make its arrival by then there were ways . . .

Hadn't her grandmother once mentioned something about a swig of castor oil and a very bumpy buggy ride?

"Excuse me, Shirley," the receptionist at the front desk asked as Shirley was waddling her way toward the exit. "When did the doctor say he wanted to see you again?"

"Next week," she answered.

The woman looked at Shirley sympathetically—or was it pathetically? Hard to tell.

"How about next Monday at ten a.m.?" the receptionist suggested. "It's the day after Mother's Day."

Shirley sighed as if to say, *Don't remind me*. Instead she responded, "How appropriate."

Later that afternoon Shirley was faced with the hearts, flowers, and chocolates of Mother's Day. She stood in the middle of the mall surrounded by a zillion reminders that it was once again time to pay homage to women with wombs.

Mothers.

Strange creatures.

Even though her current bloated condition and three living testaments at home qualified her as the recipient of such tribute, Shirley felt oddly detached from the masses honored one day each year.

It was the day Shirley dreaded.

Loathed was more like it.

Maybe this year she would let Stan baby-sit while she went to the marathon movie theater. Nope. Couldn't sit that long. Maybe she'd go to the local pub and play pool. That was out, too. In her shape, Shirley couldn't manage her belly up to the table to shoot.

Oh, well . . .

Perhaps she could just feign the flu and slumber through those twenty-four hours. But she knew she could not do that, either. No. Shirley would have to remain awake to fully experience the fever, nausea, and pain of that blessed day.

For a moment Shirley almost forgot why she was surrounded by the insanity of the season and the madness of the mall. She had come to honor her own list of women—the mothers in her life.

But first things first. There was a baby sleeping on her bladder.

"Could you please tell me where the nearest rest room is?" Shirley asked someone who was sure to know—a woman pushing a stroller with one hand while dragging a toddler with the other.

The woman nodded to the left. "In the back of the bookstore right over there."

"Thanks. That's where I'm headed anyway."

Once nature's call was answered, Shirley knew she had another good thirteen minutes before it sounded again.

She headed straight toward the travel book section. She was shopping for her own mother, Lena, with whom Shirley was finally beginning to share validation after thirty-some years of being mother and daughter.

It was usually a bore to shop for her mom, but this year

Shirley was glad for the can't-miss custom that had been established way back when Shirley was a teenager. Lena would select her own present and all Shirley had to do was go pay for it.

This year it was a book about Hawaii. Why Hawaii, Shirley had no clue. Her mother was afraid of ships and planes. While standing in the cashier's line, Shirley began thumbing through the pages. It was filled with colorful photos of teenie-weenie bronzed women clad in string bikinis sprawled on white sandy beaches. "One of my thighs weighs more than two of those beach bimbos," Shirley muttered aloud.

"Did you say something?" the man ahead of her in line asked.

"Yes, would you please hold this and save my place?" Shirley shoved the book at him and headed back toward the rest room.

Next on the list came Stan's mother. The mother of all mothers-in-law. She and Shirley were not exactly friends, but they were not foes, either. In fact, Shirley's feelings for the woman fluctuated regularly. She was, after all, Stan's mother and the grandmother of their children. Oh, well, that was a different subject altogether, and for the moment, Shirley had to stay focused on the task at hand.

"May I help you with something?" the department store clerk inquired.

"I'm looking for a gift for my mother-in-law."

"How about chocolates? We sell some of the finest in the world."

Shirley shook her head. "No. I always choose ones with the wrong nugget centers."

"How about clothes? Every woman loves a new outfit, and we're having a great sale in the ladies' department upstairs."

"Clothes won't work," Shirley said. "My mother-in-law

is roughly the size of our living room, but she is always insulted by the size we guess. Besides, the color is *always* wrong."

"Have you considered perfume? One size fits all."

"Uh-uh. It doesn't matter what Elizabeth Taylor says, my mother-in-law thinks any of the perfumes I choose stink!"

The clerk finally chuckled and smiled knowingly. "I understand. I did my mother-in-law shopping yesterday."

"What did you buy?" Shirley asked eagerly.

"A gift certificate."

She paused for a moment, trying to think of ways her mother in-law could find fault with a gift certificate. "Great idea," she concluded. "I'll take one.

Enough energy expended on her mother-in-law. Why hadn't she gone generic and bought gift certificates for every birthday, Christmas, and Mother's Day during the past decade and a half?

Shirley now shifted her attention, as well as her belly. The baby had nestled off to one side, causing Shirley to shift to one side as if one leg was four inches shorter than the other. She did her best to be inconspicuous in the middle of the mall, lacing her fingers together and hoisting the bottom of her belly from right to left. "Better," she groaned, and continued hobbling through the mall.

She had two grandmothers to shop for. Stan's grandma was a delight. No matter what she received, she did so with joy and appreciation. The kids could glue marshmallows to a piece of paper and she would act just as thrilled as the year the family bought her a new television set.

Shirley finally opted for a phone with extra-large glow-in-the dark lighted numbers and a red lighted button for numbers that were preprogrammed. They had tried a telephone once before with emergency and frequently-called numbers preprogrammed, but Grandma's eyesight was failing, so the three or four times a week when she tried to call Stan's family, she got the fire department instead.

Shirley suspected Grandma liked all of the attention, because there were always freshly baked brownies when the firemen arrived.

Shirley's own grandmother, Clara, was not so easy to shop for. She lived in a retirement center, or "old folks" home as she called it, confined by a broken arthritic hip to a wheelchair the woman detested. Shirley's grandmother had been a USO entertainer during World War II. She had traveled the world bringing joy and laughter to people who really needed it. Now from her wheelchair she continued to pound the piano every now and then and to belt out a tune or two to help cheer her fellow "inmates." But those tunes were coming less and less frequently.

Clara had been a single parent when single parents weren't very common. She had given Lena everything a mother could give a daughter, and yet comparing the two women was like comparing sand to sugar, sugar not being Lena.

Shirley's childhood memories of her grandmother Clara were visiting her on the one-acre lot Clara called a farm. She even had an old Jersey cow that the neighbor boy came over to milk twice a day. A real pioneer woman.

Maybe Shirley could buy her a book about cows. Those black-and-white cows were all the rage. No. Books were out. Clara could not see well enough to read, and did not like "stories on tapes." "It makes me feel like a little child who doesn't yet know how to read, so someone has to do it for me," she bemoaned. Shirley didn't see what was wrong with feeling like a child and being pampered, but Shirley's grandmother lived to do for others, and didn't like it when she was on the receiving end. Shirley could understand— doing for others gave the doer power. Being the one who was on the receiving end was an altogether different experience. Shirley knew there had to be a balance, but for now, Shirley was glad she was not the one who was "done for."

I really should drive clear out to the retirement center and visit her myself, thought Shirley. Giving of oneself was so much more meaningful. It was also so much more time-consuming. After the baby is born. I'll take the kid and we'll go visit Clara. Maybe I'll make her some gumbo. Grandma loves cajun food, and that would be a gift of self—sort of, since Clara was the one who taught Shirley how to cook in the first place. Not that Shirley was any great cook, but most of her core talents could be traced back to someone special in her life—someone who had taken the time to mother her in one way or another.

Shirley finally decided on a CD of Frank Sinatra's greatest hits. If Gran won't like it, her friends probably will.

Shirley also ordered flowers to be delivered on Saturday so they'd be fresh for Mother's Day. She got a little carried away and sent them to both grandmothers and six other women Shirley and her family had been mothered by. Among them were a neighbor, two women from church, and each of her children's homeroom teachers.

The biggest, brightest bouquet went to Nellie Gleed, their neighbor and a surrogate mother to each member of Shirley's family. The woman was a dynamo. At nearly ninety, she had the get-up-and-go of a dozen younger women. Last Shirley heard, she was planning her second whitewater excursion down Snake River in Wyoming. Nellie was an inspiration to all who met her and had done everything from dipping homemade chocolates to tying homemade quilts for Shirley and her family. There was a woman who knew who how to give the gifts that kept on giving. Giving of herself.

Someday Shirley would be the same kind of woman. She'd dip homemade chocolates. Learn to sew. Give her heart-made creation to others. But not now. Not for a while. After the baby is born . . .

* * *

Shirley then headed back to the bookstore rest room and decided to do a little shopping for herself. She splurged. She bought a book on successful parenting, more because she was curious to know what *defined* successful parenting than for any skills she hoped to acquire at this point in the game. She stopped by her favorite candy story and bought a couple of boxes of candy, just in case she had forgotten someone. She found a maternity store and bought a new bra—one that promised extra paneled support and a nifty opening for nursing mothers.

That was one good thing about being pregnant—she finally managed a chest of sorts. Too bad the only time I get a chest is when my belly protrudes beyond my boobs. *Real* attractive, she thought.

She bought a new soft and flowing, but tent-sized, nightgown, equipped with windows for nursing mothers. It had only been four years since her last baby, but somehow Shirley's mind had blanked out all of the little reminders of pregnancy. Swollen leaking breasts, swollen sore ankles, and a swollen face that men liked to refer to as "radiant." And how could she forget a forever swollen bladder? She couldn't.

The thought was enough to send her back to the bookstore rest room.

Shirley could not help it. Once she started shopping, she had to remember *everyone* in the family. She knew the price she would pay when she got home if anyone was forgotten. Stan got a box of candy turtles, the kind made of milk chocolate, caramel, and pecans. They were Shirley's favorites.

Thirteen-year-old Samantha got a new pair of jeans. It didn't matter how many she had or that they all looked exactly alike, Sami never had enough. Shirley knew she would score extra points with her daughter if she bought the outrageously priced, torn, and ragged-looking brand.

Shirley had to convince herself that she was investing in a relationship with her maturing daughter, not being ripped off by the ripped pair of designer denim pants.

Nine-year-old Sean got a ball made of some weird sticky type of rubber so that when he threw it against his bedroom wall, it stuck. Shirley wasn't too happy with herself for that choice. But by tomorrow afternoon, it would be in the trash. What a waste. Still, she kept buying stupid little faddish toys one day, only to find herself bending over to pick them up off the floor the next day to toss them in the garbage. Mothers really were crazy.

Four-year-old Sara was a lot like Gran. She was happy just as long as she was remembered. The price tag or the name brand still didn't matter to her. What she really wanted was a turtle. A living, breathing, stinking, slimy reptile. Instead, Shirley bought a bow for her hair. It was green. She'd tell her it resembled a turtle and she'd share one of Stan's candy turtles with her. If she did it before dinner, she might be able to pull it off without too much trauma.

With every purchase, the trip up and down the entire mall and ultimately out to the car, looked more and more like it was not going to happen. Shirley had to keep stopping to rearrange her accumulating packages as the baby decided to try out all sorts of new gymnastics techniques.

Shirley bit her lip, aghast at the thought that her water might break and she would go into labor in the middle of the jam-packed mall. If she had been in the grocery store, she knew just what to do. Break a jar of pickles and waddle out unnoticed. But here? How was she going to explain . . .

The baby did some sort of triple-somersault and Shirley *knew* she had to get out NOW.

If she weren't so panicked, she never would have done it. She would have taken the long, safe way out to the parking lot. Instead, Shirley opted for the short cut.

She forgot about the revolving doors until it was too late.

"Help!" she cried out when she realized she was stuck.

Really stuck. Crammed in one of those little triangular glassed-in push-your-way out cubies. Shirley, her belly, and eleven packages of varying sizes were all crammed in as neatly as dill pickles in a jar. The image of pickles reminded her of breaking a jar in a grocery store to camouflage her broken water—it was a trick that she'd heard of in some sitcom, but just the image made her force her knees together. Okay, maybe not really *together*, but at least in the same direction.

"Help!" she cried again. At this point embarrassment gave way to full-blown claustrophobia.

The faces of strangers, young and old, gawked at Shirley as if they'd discovered a trapped alien, but no human hand reached to rescue her. Not until Shirley heard the voice of a woman. A woman clearly in charge.

"Get out of the way!" the voice commanded. "Can't you see this woman needs help?"

The crowd parted and a woman dressed in a flowing forrest-green cloak knelt down, dislodged the paper shopping bag that was wedged beneath the door, and released a nearly hyperventilating, but extraordinarily grateful, Shirley.

"Are you all right?" the woman asked once they were free from the crowd and as safe as one can be on the sidewalk outside a mall.

"I'll be okay now. Thank you for rescuing me. I feel like such an idiot," Shirley blubbered. " I am totally humiliated. I don't know what I was thinking. I'm as big as a heifer. I should have never attempted to—"

"Will you *stop*?" The woman laughed. "Actually, it was the highlight of my day."

Shirley looked at her rescuer for the first time. Pencil-thin. Early forties. The auburn highlights were not from any sun in this universe. And the makeup—a little overdone, but applied meticulously. The clothes were nice. Real silk—from the fat worms in China, not from the skinny silk worms at Wal-Mart. One glance saw that her nails were manicured professionally, her black pumps were new. The jewelry was genuine 14-karat, probably even 24, and there was no wedding band on the left hand.

Shirley must have stared a little too long.

"I didn't mean to make you uncomfortable," said the woman sincerely.

"It's a little late for that." Shirley laughed, too. "But my discomfort has nothing to do with you. Thank you so much for coming to my aid. I think the rest of the shoppers would have turned me into an amusement attraction. The creature from The Planet Bloat."

The woman smiled, revealing shiny white teeth. Orthodontia had obviously improved on Mother Nature's original plan—no one had ever grown such uniform perfection without the aid of a high-priced orthodontist. She had probably worn braces for years. Everything about the woman was Hollywood-perfect. Maybe she was a movie star. Shirley stared. If she wasn't, she could have been.

"Can I help you to your car?" the woman offered.

Shirley handed her the largest and most awkward bags. "Thanks. I don't know you, do I?"

The auburn curls shifted from side to side. "My name is Rita. I just moved to town. The big divorce, you know."

Shirley readjusted her load and stuck out a hand. "Hi. I'm Shirley—the big mother lode."

Both women laughed in unison, and Shirley couldn't help thinking that she did know this glamorous woman after all.

Before they parted, Shirley had given Rita her telephone number and invited her to lunch. She really hoped Rita would call. She and Shirley could not have been more different, but Shirley was in need of a good friend, not to mention a good lunch.

Two

Shirley was ten minutes late picking Sara up from preschool.

"Did you forget about me, Mommy?"

"Of course not, sweetie. I just got *stuck* at the mall." The thought made Shirley smile.

"I made a surprise for you for Mother's Day," Sara announced proudly.

Shirley grinned. "Really? What is it?"

"I can't tell. It's a surprise."

"Those are my favorite Mother's Day presents," Shirley lied, like any good mother would.

Later that night, after macaroni-and-cheese casserole *again*, and after the kids received their gifts from her impromptu guilt-driven shopping spree, Shirley lay on top of her bed, too tired to get off, pull down the covers and crawl in properly. Every inch of her body ached. Screamed for relief. She reached for the box of turtles she had given Stan.

"How did your doctor's appointment go?" Stan asked, flopping down on the bed just hard enough to jolt every one of Shirley's just-beginning-to-relax muscles.

"Everything's right on target."

"No problems?"

His tone alarmed Shirley. "What do you mean?"

"I mean the water retention. Isn't that a concern?"

"I didn't know you were so aware of my water level."

Her feeling of alarm quickly turned to annoyance. "I'm fine. Just pregnant."

"What about the irritability?"

"*What* irritability?" she snapped.

Stan reached for a chocolate, but Shirley snapped the lid closed.

After surviving three pregnancies, the man hadn't learned a thing. "And what did the doctor say about your weight gain? Aren't they worried about high blood pressure?"

Shirley took a deep breath, or at least she tried to. Then her bare feet landed in the square of Stan's back. He was on the floor before he knew it.

"What was *that* all about?" He seemed genuinely bewildered as he staggered to his feet.

"Just chalk it up to my water retention, irritability, and weight gain!" she said, popping a whole turtle into her mouth.

Sometime after she fell asleep, the phone rang. And rang. And rang.

Finally someone picked it up, and somewhere in the depths of slumber, Shirley heard Stan bellow from downstairs, "Shirley, it's for you."

"Hello," Shirley muttered as she fumbled with the receiver.

"Hi, Shirley. It's Rita. I hope I didn't wake you."

It took at least ten seconds for Shirley to remember who Rita was. Then she looked at her clock on the nightstand. It was only 9:00 P.M. But it felt like it was 3:00 A.M. "Oh, no. I wasn't sleeping," Shirley lied.

"I just called to see if tomorrow would be a good day to take you up on your offer for lunch. My office is being painted and I'm all unpacked, so I thought . . ."

"Sure. Tomorrow sounds great." The idea of a lunch she didn't spread on a piece of bread brought Shirley to full-alert status. Besides, Rita was intriguing and Shirley was up for a little intrigue. "What if we meet at The Garden? It's a soup and salad place on Main Street."

"The Garden is fine, but why don't you let me come and pick you up? That way you won't have to worry about driving in your condition." Rita laughed, a little hesitantly. "I hope I didn't offend you."

"You didn't," Shirley assured her. "I don't take offense. I give it. Just ask my husband, Stan, who blames my snarly moods on my 'condition,' even when I'm not pregnant." She laughed at her own joke.

The next morning, Shirley got up early to clean the house. She swept the kitchen and bathroom floors and ran a wet mop over them. She washed dishes and put a fresh cloth on the kitchen table. She sprayed some floral potpourri and lit a cinnamon candle. She thought about vacuuming, but decided against it. No use going into labor before lunch.

Stan kissed her carefully on the cheek. "Good morning. It looks like you're getting serious about having this baby. You're nesting."

"I'm not nesting. I'm just cleaning. I want the house to look nice when my new friend gets here."

"You mean the woman who called you last night? Isn't she the one who pried you out of the revolving door?"

Why did Shirley have to tell him everything? It always came back to haunt her. "That's the one. We're going to lunch. So if you'll take Sara to preschool, I'll pick her up."

"Sure," said Stan. "No problem. I can even pick her up if you would like more time to spend with . . . what did you say your friend's name was?"

"Rita. And why are you being so nice?" she asked suspiciously, knowing that after her behavior last night, Stan did not need to be nice to her. She had apologized for kicking him in the back, but he had just laughed and blamed it on her "condition."

Now Stan picked up a wet dishcloth and ran it over the

top of the fridge. "I'm not being nice. I'm just nesting. *We're* about to have a baby."

"Sometimes I love you," she said, backing into his chest because she couldn't manage a tight enough hug facing him.

He wrapped his arms nearly all the way around her and patted her stomach.

"I love you more today than I did yesterday," she said.

Stan kissed her neck. "Yeah, but yesterday you hated my guts!"

Lunch consisted of Jamaican black bean soup and all the iceberg lettuce you could eat.

"This is a quaint little cafe," said Rita, buttering a soda cracker with the real artery-clogging stuff.

"Charming, isn't it? You know, I didn't think you and I could ever be friends," Shirley confessed.

"Why?"

"Because you're too skinny. That's the first thing I noticed about you."

Rita laughed. "I presume you took note of my weight after you were freed from the revolving door. But actually, I'm not slender enough to be noticeable."

"No, I mean it. Call me prejudiced, but lately skinny people really *bug* me. Rickets isn't a contagious disease, is it?" Shirley teased.

Rita continued laughing. "Shirley, I might not be the best thing for you, but you certainly are a blessing to me."

Shirley had a million questions she wanted to ask Rita. Her natural curiosity demanded to know all the juicy details of Rita's life, including her briefly mentioned recent divorce. However, Rita was driving and Shirley wanted to make sure she still had a ride home. So she kept the queries simple.

"Why did you decide to settle here in our illustrious little city?"

"I do a lot of social work. Right now, I've decided to open a public relations firm for nonprofit organizations. The demographics here are favorable."

Shirley stuck a big spoonful of soup into her mouth, but her eyes still questioned, "Huh?" She suddenly felt very uneducated and small-town, so she followed the soup with a big bite of lettuce, thinking that if she kept eating, she would not say anything stupid in front of this woman who obviously was the epitome of sophistication. Shirley couldn't help feeling not only inferior, but somewhat envious.

"I guess what really drew me here," Rita's lip began to quiver as the model of sophistication fought to maintain her composure, "is the fact that I have absolutely no ties here. No ex-husbands and none of their mistresses. No coworkers who saw me fall apart. No family and no friends to keep reminding me that I have failed miserably at the most important ventures of my life."

Shirley wasn't sure whether or not a response was required. Did Rita say *husbands*? Shirley was dying to ask how many and all about those dissolved marriages, but suspected that what Rita really needed was not a barrage of questions, but simply a sounding board. So Shirley did what any true friend does— she listened.

It wasn't easy for Shirley, but she kept alternating bites of soup and chunks of lettuce, just to ensure her own silence, as Rita poured out her soul. She talked of a life of affluence and apocalypse. Deceit and disappointment. A princess broken. She spoke in general terms while Shirley craved details, but refrained from querying.

It was a life so foreign to Shirley that it might as well have been a work of fiction. A soap opera. But it wasn't. It was real. Rita was born into a family of old money and power. She was educated, traveled, and regal. But right now, she was on the brink of breaking down in front of a near-stranger.

Rita sniffled and wiped her eyes with the corner of her napkin. "I guess I'm evidence that money does not buy happiness."

Shirley had heard that line too many times. "From one who has six dollars and nine cents in her checking account, I'd say you just didn't know where to shop!"

"How was your lunch?" Stan asked early that evening while husband and wife were out on their weekly "get away from the kids" date. They were doing some joint grocery shopping.

"I can still taste it." Shirley burped. "Excuse me."

"Tell me about your friend Rita. She comes from money, huh?"

Shirley instantly felt defensive. "Yeah, but so what? There is a lot more to her than her bank account."

"Sorry. I didn't mean to imply anything derogatory."

"*I'm* sorry, hon. It's just that I feel Rita and I have been friends forever. It's one of those rare, rare connections. Kinda like you and me—the connection defies logic."

Stan helped Shirley lift a box of laundry detergent into their cart. "Should I be jealous?"

Shirley chuckled. "Hardly."

"So tell me about Rita," said Stan, trying to sneak a box of Twinkies into the cart without Shirley detecting them.

Shirley tossed a second box of Twinkies into the cart. "She is one of the warmest and funniest people I've ever met. After she stopped crying, we laughed until I almost peed my pants."

Stan muttered, "That wouldn't take much these days."

"What did you say?"

"I said I need something for lunch Tuesday."

Shirley gave him that sideways "Yeah, right" look, but continued her Rita story. "Her family is from the Northwest. They are spread between Seattle and Portland. She's been educated in the best schools in the U.S. and Europe.

She's traveled the world. I think she married young. Her father really liked her first husband. I think it was one of those archaic forced unions."

"Her *first* husband?" Stan questioned, tossing a package of toilet paper at Shirley.

She caught it and threw it into the cart. "Yeah. I know she's been married at least twice."

"At *least*?"

"I know her last husband was a doctor who became more interested in the anatomy of student nurses than in anatomy in general. Can you believe men, it doesn't matter whether they are doctors or ditch-diggers, they're all the same."

Stan stood in front of a rack of two hundred loaves of bread, pretending to be perplexed by the variety. When Shirley finally stopped talking, he reached for a loaf of sourdough.

"So why *is* she here?" he asked.

Shirley lifted her shoulders. "I'm not sure. I suspect it's because this is an easy place in which to lose yourself."

Stan double-checked the shopping list. "How come you didn't write down any of the good stuff, like chips and dip or frozen pizzas?"

"Because I'm trying to diet."

"Which one is it this week, all grapefruit, whole grain, all protein, no sugar, no carbs, no taste?"

Shirley shook her head and returned the loaf of sourdough to the bread shelf. "No white bread."

Stan put it back in the cart. "Just because you're dieting, doesn't mean the rest of us are. I'm not sure it's a good idea for you to diet while you're pregnant anyway."

"It's nothing radical. Just a few smart choices to help me keep my weight under control."

Stan coughed. Or was it a snort?

"Are you laughing at me?"

He looked like a five-year-old caught with his hand in his mother's purse. "Why would I laugh at you?"

"Because maybe, just maybe, you think my pregnancy weight is *already* out of control." There were a few issues in Shirley's life that she was hypersensitive about—her weight covered the first five of the top-ten list.

"Shirl, don't worry at this point—just go ahead for the next few weeks and splurge. After the baby comes, we'll diet and exercise together."

After the baby comes . . .

Three

They were back in the car with all of the grocery bags neatly stacked in the backseat when Shirley resumed their original conversation. "Rita has done a lot of social work and now she has opened up a public relations firm to help all types of charities."

"Sounds like a noble cause."

"Rita's a noble woman. I know she's financially set, so she does not *have* to work, but she wants to make her life mean something. She is totally devoted to the underprivileged."

"Have you asked her for a handout yet?"

"The only hand 'out' you're going to get is this one!" she teased Stan, pushing his shoulder. "You know what they say, 'If you're looking for a hand, you'll find it at the end of your arm.'"

Stan tossed his head back and laughed so hard, his belly shook like Santa's. "Will this arm do?" he asked, pulling her closer.

Shirley laid her head on her husband's shoulder. "Maybe grocery shopping isn't the dry date it sounds like. It has its moments."

They drove for a while, enjoying the silence. It was a rare commodity around home.

"Your friend Rita sounds like a great lady," Stan said after a few miles. "What does she look like?" Before he had even said it, he felt his foot heading directly for his mouth.

Shirley bolted forward, the safety belt cutting across her front. "What does that have to do with anything?" Shirley knew it was one thing for her to observe Rita from head to toe; it was quite *another* for Stan to do the same.

"Sorry. Sorry," Stan apologized. "I just mean . . . how old is she?"

"What?"

"It wasn't like I asked her measurements!" he made a feeble attempt to defend himself.

Shirley's mouth fell open in feigned shock. "What is the matter with you, Stan?"

Stan felt his foot wedge further down his throat. He knew if he kept going on with this line of questioning, he'd soon be gnawing off his own appendage. "What I meant to ask is, does Rita have kids?"

"I don't think so," answered Shirley. "She lives in a condo in the heart of the city. She never mentioned children. I had a million questions to ask about her personal life, but I didn't want to pry."

This time it was Stan's turn to feign shock. "Since when?"

"Not funny, honey. Why did you ask whether or not she has kids?"

"I thought it might be nice to invite Rita to dinner on Mother's Day."

"You're not going to make me cook *again* this year, are you?"

"No, I'm not."

"Then you're going to be sticking that pot roast in the oven?"

"No, I'm not."

"So where are we dining out?"

He knew he was again headed into dangerous territory. "Why don't you make reservations at that new bistro down on the waterfront that we've been wanting to try?"

Shirley smiled. Things were looking brighter. "It's Mother's Day. Why don't *you* make the reservations and let me just lay back and bask like all of the other beached walruses?"

Stan reached over and squeezed his wife's knee affectionately. "Tell you what. I'll take care of every detail on Mother's Day. You don't have to worry about a thing. You can stay in bed until it's time to go to dinner. Give your friend Rita a call and invite her, then leave all the tributes to motherhood to your old man."

Shirley let her head fall back against the headrest. She did her best to imagine what Mother's Day would be like if Stan took over all of her responsibilities. The thought terrified her and she jerked forward, the safety belt again snapping around her bulging midsection.

"I can't expect you to take care of everything. It's a sweet thought, but somebody has to make sure the gifts are delivered to our mothers. And our grandmothers. Flowers for everybody, even the kids' teachers, will have to be delivered on Saturday. And we can't forget sweet little Mrs. Gleed down the street. We always include her in our family activities."

Stan reached over and loosen her safety belt. "I love Mrs. Gleed. Can't she come to dinner with us?"

"I'd love to invite her, but I'm sure she's celebrating with her own family. She's got more people devoted to her than the Pope."

"Can you imagine how desperately miserable Mother's Day would be if you didn't have a family?"

Shirley contemplated his question. She knew what he was saying, and felt for the women who were left to fend for themselves on this most sacred day, but the thought of spending it alone didn't seem all that miserable to Shirley.

"You *do* realize Mother's Day is on Sunday?" she reminded Stan. "That means church. Sara is singing in the children's chorus. Sean needs a haircut. And he'll have to wear his new suit because he's been asked to help pass out the little planters given to every woman in the congregation. Samantha has a speaking assignment. She won't tell me what it's about, but the pastor asked her weeks ago. I think it's a tribute to me. Did I mention Sara is singing in the children's chorus?"

"Enough already!" Stan laughed. "The whole world would shut down if you were out of commission for a day, wouldn't it?"

"I don't know about the entire world, but *your* world certainly would spin out of its orbit."

Shirley cuddled against Stan and allowed herself to relax and enjoy the three minutes remaining of the ride home.

"I feel sleepy." She yawned.

Stan carried in all of the groceries and had done his best to put them away before he woke his wife.

That evening after her catnap and dinner, Shirley was in the middle of a game of Monopoly with the kids when it was her turn to toss the dice. Two hotels and three houses went flying off the board and across the kitchen.

"Mom!" bellowed Sean, owner of the hotels. "Don't throw so hard."

Samantha looked at Shirley's ashen face and whispered, "What's wrong, Mom?"

Through clenched teeth, Shirley managed, "Contraction."

The kids immediately jumped into action. Sara shouted at the top of her lungs, "Is the baby coming? Is the baby coming? Help! The baby's coming! Somebody get Mom a glass of boiling water!"

"What for?" Sean demanded.

"Because a lady having a baby always needs boiling water."

"She does?"

Sara rolled her eyes. "Yes. I saw it on TV."

Sean shook his head, pushed his little sister out of the way and whispered, "Am I supposed to boil water for you, Mom?"

"No." Shirley grimaced, squeezing his hand until his knuckles popped. "Everything you see on TV doesn't match up with real life."

"What do you want me to do?" he asked, trying to pry his fingers free of her grip.

Samantha was standing behind him. "Yeah, Mom, what should we do?"

"What a night for Stan to have to go into the office! Call your daddy at work," Shirley instructed as soon as the contraction subsided enough for her breath to return.

Sean ran for the phone. Samantha pressed her hand against Shirley's clammy forehead. Sara grabbed the car keys.

"Let's go to the hospital and get that thing outta your tummy, Mommy. Come on. Let's go. Let's go." Sara tugged at Shirley, who was bracing for another contraction.

"There's no answer at Dad's office so I left an emergency message," Sean announced. "Maybe he's already on his way home."

"I don't think Mom can wait," said Samantha, ever the nurse. "Maybe we should boil some water. It was on *General Hospital,* so it might be the right thing to do."

That made Shirley laugh. When she laughed, she relaxed. When she relaxed, the contractions subsided.

By the time Stan raced through the front door, an hour later, Shirley and the kids were sound asleep in front of the TV.

False alarm.

The next morning found Shirley indeed nesting. She disposed of all the unidentifiable fur balls growing in the fridge.

"What's *this*?" Shirley asked Samantha.

Samantha looked into the container her mother held out. "Yuck! It's purple-and-green stuff."

"I think it's supposed to be cottage cheese," offered Stan, after venturing a look.

"Aged cottage cheese, maybe," Shirley said, launching it into the garbage can. "Do you realize how disgusting our family is?"

They both nodded.

After the fridge, Shirley went through her underwear drawer and threw out everything that was stained, frayed, or dingy.

"How come you're throwing all of your underwear in the garbage?" Sara wanted to know.

"Because when I was a little girl, my mother, your grandma Lena, told me that I should never, ever wear a pair of underwear that wasn't clean—just in case of an accident."

Sara scrunched up her little nose in confusion. "But, Mommy, if you had an accident, the underwear you had on wouldn't be very clean."

"Good point, honey."

Shirley smiled and stroked her daughter's curls. Then she tossed the last remaining pair away, wondering if they were pink by design or by accident. She made a mental note to hit the lingerie store, because there was not one pair in the entire drawer that would have passed Lena's "just in case of an accident" inspection.

She wiped away the pictures Sara had drawn in the dust on the coffee table, and used the hand-held vacuum to suck up two bags of potato chips from under the couch cushions.

Once a week, Shirley had a girl come in to help with the housework, but Shirley always cleaned before she arrived. No way she could have the maid find a mess.

Shirley tried Rita at both of the numbers she had given. There was no answer at home, and the office number still wasn't connected. She's a busy woman of the world, thought Shirley as she sat down at the kitchen table to color with Sara.

"Draw all the animals in Noah's ark," instructed Sara.

"You tell me which ones you want."

"How about a horse?"

Shirley selected a brown crayon and did her best to draw a horse. There was a head, a tail, four legs, and a mane.

Sara looked at her mother's work with innocent disdain. "I said I wanted a horse," she whined.

"It *is* a horse."

"But it's fat and funny-looking."

Shirley stuck out her lower lip and pretended her feelings were hurt. "It's the best horse Mommy knows how to draw."

Sara's tender heart did not want to wound her mother's artistic feelings. "I know," she said, her eyes lighting up like Christmas bulbs. "It *is* a horse! It's just fat and funny-looking because it's *pregnant*!"

By afternoon, Shirley was ready to say good night. She had answered the phone at least a dozen times. The first call was from her mother, who was eager to move in and take over the minute Shirley was admitted to the hospital. Shirley knew two things: Her children would be well-fed, and her cupboards would be rearranged when she returned.

"You realize, women in my day stayed in bed at least a month after having a baby," Lena said.

"Sounds good to me, Mom. I could use a month's worth of rest. I'm just glad I don't have to worry about my family while I'm in the hospital. I hope you know how much we appreciate all you do for us."

"Oh, I know you kids do. But mothers can never do too much for their children."

Shirley wanted desperately to disagree with a vengeance. She just didn't have the energy. She'd given it all to her children.

* * *

Shirley's mother-in-law had also been one of the callers. She always began each conversation with "Hi."

That was it.

Shirley was expected to take it from there. The woman never identified herself. She never started the conversation with a question like "How are you?" She just said "Hi," and sat in silence. Shirley was expected to guess who she was and what she wanted. It annoyed Shirley, but it also bothered her that her mother-in-law never asked how Stan, Shirley, or the children were doing. Today, after Shirley took over with "Hello, Mother. How are you doing?" the woman mentioned something about the weather and then launched into a tirade about her sagging bladder.

"It's completely shot," she announced. "I can't drink a half cup of tea without having to run down the hallway."

The hint of suggestion got to Shirley.

"Hold on for a second," Shirley said, "I'll be right back." When she returned from the bathroom, her mother-in-law was kind enough to apprise Shirley of the state of her slipped disc, her itchy hemorrhoids, and her plaguing constipation.

"I'm so sorry you're not feeling well."

"It's nothing to trouble you about. It's just old age. Besides, you aren't close enough to do much about my failing health."

"Mother, we just live on the other side of town."

"Well, it's not like I see you often enough to remember what those kids look like."

"We saw you last weekend. Remember?"

"That's right. That's right. I'd forgotten. Oh well, did I tell you the doctor took away my high blood pressure medication? The nerve of that man. Said I didn't need it. How does he know what I need?"

"How's Dad doing?" Shirley attempted a quick change of subject.

Her mother-in-law groaned. "He's old, and he *acts* old.

He's always complaining about every ache and pain. You can't believe how that wears on my nerves."

"Can't imagine." Shirley smiled. She could hear her dear, sweet father-in-law's voice in the background. "What's Dad saying?"

"Oh, nothing of consequence. He's just asking how you all are doing."

"Tell him we're just fine, Mother. Please call again soon. It's always such a pleasure."

There were also the sales calls, the wrong numbers, and the calls for Stan and the children. The twelfth call of the day was from Rita.

"I just rang you up to thank you for lunch. I thought it was fun, but you must think I'm a lunatic."

"I like lunatics," said Shirley. "I surround myself with them."

"Thanks for letting me join the throng," said Rita, sounding genuinely grateful. "After you give birth, we'll have to do lunch again. I promise to be better composed."

"After I 'give birth,' I'm not making any promises about my composure. But before the big event, why don't you come and join our family for dinner on Mother's Day? Stan says he'll spring for the festivities."

There was a long pause before Rita responded. "Mother's Day? I'm sorry. I can't. It's kind of you to ask, but I just won't be able to make it."

She hung up before Shirley had a chance to protest.

Four

It was just before midnight when Shirley awoke with a start. A kick start. She vaguely remembered someone helping her up the stairs to bed. Now she nudged the lump that was lying next to her. It didn't budge.

She elbowed it again. This time it grunted.

"I'm miserable," she whined into the darkness.

Stan finally groaned. "It's the middle of the night. Can't this wait till morning?"

Was this the caring, sensitive man who had vowed to love her, cherish her through sickness and health? No. It was Stan.

She jabbed him again. "Wake up. It's the baby."

Reality registered. Stan rolled over and put his hand on Shirley's protruding belly. "Is it time?"

"No. No. It's not that," said Shirley, struggling to obtain an upright position. "I'm just miserable. I feel rotten. The baby is kicking so hard, my ribs are about to break. My legs are cramped. My back aches. My boobs are about to explode."

"Shirley, I'm sorry. I feel for you. I really do. But let's go back to sleep."

"How can I sleep when I'm like this?"

"Roll over and lay on your stomach this time," he instructed. "You snore when you're lying on your back."

Shirley hadn't been able to roll over, let alone lie on her

stomach for months. "Roll over. You make me sound like a trained puppy."

"Well, it's better than sounding like my mother."

She knew she should have been furious. She was just too miserable to pick a fight. "I'm back to that *can't stand you* feeling. In case you are wondering."

No comment from the lump who was now curled up on the other side of the bed as far away as he could get without going over the edge.

"I have to pee," Shirley announced.

No comment.

She managed to dangle her feet off the side of the bed. The counterweight worked like a charm and her body bolted upright. Still no movement from the lump. It was only when Shirley flipped the light switch on that Stan groaned and pulled the covers up over his head.

"How did you sleep?" Stan asked cautiously the next morning.

Shirley shot him a glare that could have seared a side of beef.

"Sorry," he said. "Can I fix you anything for breakfast?" He looked a little pitiful standing there in his Mr. Magoo boxers stirring frozen juice, trying to make amends.

It was so hard for Shirley to hold a grudge after the sun came up. Anger at night was always easier for her to maintain, and this morning, Shirley wasn't much in the mood. "Thanks. I'd like Belgian waffles with fresh berries, sweetened cream, and fresh-squeezed orange juice."

"How about Cheerios and grape juice from a can?"

"That'll do." Who did she think she was—queen of the universe? Women had been having babies since the beginning of time. What did she have to complain about? Pioneer women gave birth and drove oxen the same day. Chinese women gave birth in the middle of rice fields, without even taking a coffee break. Mother Eve had birthed the beginning of humanity, in exile, amid God's wrath and thorns and serpents.

For a fleeting moment, she felt guilty for seeking so much attention, so much pampering. She also felt grateful to be born in the glorious and enlightened day of the epidural.

They sat down at the breakfast table together. Stan reached over and put his hand on top of hers. "So what have you got planned for today?"

"I thought I'd go to the spa and do fifty laps in the pool. Get one of those European mud facials. Or . . . maybe I'll fly to our summer cottage and walk along the beach. Or . . . maybe go to first grade and be Sean's show-and-tell."

"His *show-and-tell*?"

"Don't ask. What about you, Stan? Do you have Mother's Day under control?" She wasn't going to mention it again, just let him have the responsibility and run with it. But from the panicked look on Stan's face, it was a good idea she had reminded him.

"That's all being taken care of. Don't you worry about a thing. Did you ever ask your friend Rita if she would like to join us?"

Shirley frowned. "It's strange, but when I asked her, she bolted. Almost hung up on me. I think the woman is in pain. She's got some issues."

"Do I detect a little of your psychology major in action?"

"Maybe," admitted Shirley. "It's about time I did something with that degree."

Shirley showered. She meant to shave her legs, but deemed it impossible at this point. She did manage to buzz her pits and shampoo her hair. Whoever said a pregnant woman was the most beautiful work of art had not seen Shirley naked at nine months. She still had thirteen-year-old tread marks from Samantha.

Shirley wore her Sunday maternity dress and headed out

the door with the kids. First they dropped off Samantha at junior high and then Sara at preschool. "Are you sure you still want me to do this?" she asked Sean.

"Sure I'm sure. I told you—we've been studying geometry and *nobody* else will bring a shape like *my* show-and-tell."

"I think you're right about that, son."

It wasn't as painful as Shirley had imagined. The kids were great. They all agreed that Sean's show-and-tell was the most unique shape they'd ever seen. Oval. Round. Oblong. It kept changing right before their eyes, and their pressing hands.

Three kids wanted to feel the baby move. She let them. Two asked if they could have the kid when it was born. She politely declined. One child had seen too many *Alien* movies, and ran to the bathroom in tears of terror.

Sean presented his mother with a mood pencil for her participation. It was temperature-sensitive and changed colors as you gripped it, indicating the mood you were in.

"Red means you're mad," explained Sean. "Blue means you don't care."

"Cool," said Shirley, and thanked the class.

"Let's all give Sean's mother a round of applause for being such a good sport," said the teacher and led the children in a rousing cheer.

"I hope you weren't too humiliated," she whispered as Shirley left the classroom.

"Not at all," she replied, gripping the pencil. It was bright purple.

Shirley stopped at the mall on her way home. There were a few more people she wanted to remember for Mother's Day. This time she kept the packages small and avoided the revolving door. When she pulled into her driveway, she was surprised to see Rita's car parked in front of the house.

"Hi!" said Shirley, flinging the car door open, but not

getting out because her stomach was stuck beneath the steering wheel.

"Hi," replied Rita. "I was just leaving you a note. I wanted to apologize for being so abrupt on the telephone yesterday. I told you, I'm a lunatic. Lately my emotions have been riding a roller-coaster."

Shirley shifted uncomfortably, until she felt her belly move and she was free. "Don't worry about it." She slid out sideways. "I hope this means you've changed your mind and decided to join us for Mother's Day."

"On one condition: You'll come for an afternoon ride with me."

Shirley was intrigued. She had a whole stack of work waiting for her by her computer, and the house was in need of a once over . . . okay, twice over, or even a thrice.

"Where are we going?"

"I wanted to show you my work. I think you'll find it interesting. Come on."

"Right *now*?"

"Sure. I'm just headed out to some of the project sights."

Shirley hesitated. After all, she did not know Rita that well. Maybe the woman *was* a lunatic . .

"I'll buy you lunch."

Shirley was in the car before Rita.

Five

Their first stop was at a woman's shelter not far from Shirley's house. "I didn't even know this place was here," admitted Shirley.

"Not many people do. It's supposed to be a safe place for battered women and children. If it was advertised, they wouldn't be safe."

"I see."

The building was a converted convenience store. Old. Run-down. Windows boarded. In need of a paint job. In need of a woman's touch. Shirley found the irony painful.

"Hi, Rita." An older woman dressed in black pants and a stained white T-shirt greeted them as they walked in. "We were hoping you'd be by today. The spirit is a little blue around here, this being Mother's Day weekend and everything."

Rita reached for the woman's hand and squeezed it. "I'll see what I can do." Then Rita turned to Shirley and introduced her. "This is my friend Shirley. Shirley, this is Pat, the woman in charge of this wonderful place."

Pat immediately embraced Shirley. Her warmth was genuine. "Shirley, you're welcome here."

They all chuckled at the sound of that.

There was a moment's pause and Shirley realized that Pat thought Rita had brought her here as a woman in need of a safe place. A battered woman. Well, she did feel like one—from the inside out. The baby was kicking like a linebacker.

"I'm just here visiting with Rita," Shirley explained quickly.

"Okay," said Pat. "Every woman and child is welcome here. Anytime."

Shirley patted her own protruding gut, wondering if the lump she felt was her baby's head or its other end. The kicking had not ceased.

"I come bearing the complete package—woman *and* child."

Everyone chuckled.

"I brought some books I thought the women might like," said Rita. "They're in the car. Has Dr. Memford been by yet today? He was going to try to talk to Kathy."

Pat shook her head. "He came by, but no luck. Kathy hasn't said a word since she was brought in three days ago."

"I'm so sorry. I thought he would be able to get through to her. I'll see that he keeps coming back," said Rita. "How about Phyllis? Did she get the box I sent over for her?"

"She did. She said to tell you how much she appreciated the personal hygiene items. She hadn't had a new toothbrush in as long as she could remember. And I know she really needed the diapers, formula, and baby items you sent."

Rita turned to Shirley. "You'll like Phyllis. You two have a lot in common. She's got a herd of kids, too."

Pat held up the palm of her hand. "Phyllis is gone. She left last night. Said she thought she was ready."

Shirley tried to take it all in. This was a world she had heard about on the news. A charity she donated a dollar or two to every now and then. But until this moment, a woman's shelter was not a *real* place. She felt like such an outsider, even an intruder. Rita, however, seemed very much at home. She reminded Shirley of the Rita she'd first met at the mall. A woman in charge. Here, too, she was a rescuer. But, Shirley wondered, how did Rita know Pat and the women so well if she had only been in town for a week or so?

Shirley suddenly realized that she was standing by herself. Rita and Pat were heading down a hallway and Shirley hurried to catch up to them. They turned into a doorway that lead to a big open room with military-style cots lined up against a wall. A few wooden cribs with slats missing were also there. There were no rugs on the cold tile floor. Not all of the beds had sheets, and Shirley could see the worn mattresses were stained. Blankets were a precious commodity.

There were only two people in the room. A little boy was sitting alone on one cot, clutching a worn Pooh bear that was missing one arm and still bleeding stuffing. Across from him was a hunched woman who could have been his grandmother.

The smell of the room was unlike anything Shirley had ever experienced. Dirty diapers she recognized. Bedding in need of laundering? Yes. Stale cigarette smoke? Absolutely. But the room didn't smell dirty. Maybe the odor was so pungent because she was pregnant and had a heightened sense of smell.

She even recognized the aura of musty sneakers. But there was more to it. Then Shirley saw the face of the woman. Her left eye was swollen shut, her chin purple from a deep bruise. Her two frail hands rested limp across her lamp.

The room began to shake and Shirley immediately identified the elusive smell.

Fear.

The room quaked and Shirley looked to see if the the woman was moving. Only she wasn't; it was *Shirley's* hands that were trembling.

* * *

Shirley was suddenly terrified. She wanted to run back and wait in the car with the windows rolled up and the doors safely locked. She wanted out—back into the world where she could distance herself from this place and the razor-like reality she felt cutting into her safe, sheltered soul.

For a moment she thought her knees would buckle as her mind told her body to move. Run. Run away. She stood immobile as she watched Rita approach the woman on the cot.

"Hi, Kathy. I'm Rita. Remember, I came by yesterday? I understand we have something in common. I'm the new kid on the block, too." Rita sat down next to Kathy, and the woman turned her battered face toward the wall.

Shirley stared. Now she really felt like an unwanted intruder.

"So tell me about yourself, Shirley," Pat invited, taking Shirley by the elbow and leading her across the hall to a small makeshift office. "When is your baby due?"

"About two and a half weeks."

She motioned for Shirley to sit down. "You must be excited," said Pat.

Shirley was not listening, her ears still echoed from the silence in the room across the hall. "I'm sorry?"

"I mean about the baby You must be excited about the baby. Is it your first?"

"Fourth," was all Shirley could manage, because her emotions were burning like wildfire.

"This is obviously your first visit to a woman's shelter." There was compassion in Pat's voice.

She opened a bottle of water from a case stacked next to the table she was using for a desk. She handed the bottle to Shirley, who took it gratefully, but the lump in her throat did not disappear and her hands continued to shake.

"Can I get you anything else?" Pat asked.

"No. Thank you."

"We really think the world of your friend Rita," said Pat.

"She's a human dynamo. She came in here last week, introduced herself, asked us what the shelter needed and she's already done wonders. She's quite a woman."

There was no doubt about that in Shirley's mind. After a few more minutes of chitchat, Shirley began to unwind and allowed herself to appreciate what was going on around her. She did not want to continue to feel like a stranger. This was not the depressing place she had first assumed. There was a spirit that permeated the place—a spirit of care and hope.

"Women may be victimized when they come here," explained Pat. "They may be broken and battered, but they do not remain victims for long."

"Survivors," said Shirley.

"That, and so much more."

Then Pat explained some basics to Shirley about the thirty-day program the shelter offered. Women and children in need were always taken in—no matter the circumstances. They were offered something to eat and a bed. Therapy sessions were available. That's where most of the current residents were right now—getting counsel from the so-called professionals. The children that usually accompanied the women were at an independent day care.

"Because this is a privately funded program," Pat went on, "if people don't contribute, we don't have anything to offer."

"It seems to me you have a great deal to offer."

"Thank you, but a hug and a kiss can only warm a body for so long. After that, a soft blanket and a hearty cup of soup come in handy."

"What kinds of things do you need?" asked Shirley.

"The basics, the same old things from week to week," answered Pat. "Money for rent and operating costs. Food. Clothes. Shampoo. Toothbrushes and toothpaste. Tampons. Diapers. Formula. Bedding. You name it. When these women come here, they are destitute. Very few have full suitcases.

"There are times when the balance between supply and

demand here gets a little off," admitted Pat. "But because of people like Rita, women like Kathy have a safe place to come until they can walk out of here with their dignity intact."

Shirley felt proud to know Rita, to call her a friend. She tried her best to understand all that Pat was saying, but there was just too much. She asked about Kathy. She was shocked to discover that Kathy was only twenty-four years old.

"She's been through a lot," said Pat, without disclosing any further information.

"Maybe I can help," responded Shirley. "I've got a degree in psychology." It sounded empty, even to Shirley, but the sentiment was sincere. Shirley was feeling desperate, desperate to help in any way she could.

Half an hour later, Shirley was reading to the little boy with the injured Winnie-the-Pooh bear. The child's name was Stephen, and Kathy was his mother. Shirley read a story called *Koala Lou* to the four-year-old boy, who kept his arms around Shirley's neck, his fingers laced so his embrace was secure.

"This is one of my daughter's favorite stories," said Shirley. "That's why I keep it in my purse."

The copy was tattered, but Stephen didn't mind. He wanted it read to him over and over. "I like the pictures," he said, re-adjusting his position on Shirley's lap and tightening his grip around her neck. He did his best to stay on, but kept sliding down.

"I'm sorry, sweetheart. I don't have much of a lap these days."

"That's okay, lady. Is there really a baby in your tummy?"

"There is." She placed his tiny hand on her stomach and let him feel the baby kick.

"That's neat! Is it coming out now?"

"I hope not," said Shirley.

"Can I have your baby if it's a boy?" Stephen asked openly.

Shirley smiled and stroked his hair. "Would you like a baby brother?"

Stephen's eyes suddenly overflowed with hot tears. "I had a baby brother, but he's dead now."

"Dead?"

Stephen was softly sobbing. Shirley wrapped her arms around his little body and held him close.

"He's dead. My mommy backed right over him with the car. She didn't mean to. But my daddy said it was her fault. He got real mad and beat her up. I thought she was going to die, too."

Shirley had a hard time breathing. She was sobbing along with Stephen.

"We have to stay here until my daddy's not mad anymore," Stephen continued.

Shirley could not begin to imagine the pain Kathy must be suffering, the pain little Stephen's heart held. She didn't know what to say, so she said nothing. She just held him, hugged him, and cried with him.

Once Shirley and Rita were back in the car, Rita turned to her. "I'm sorry I neglected you like that."

"Don't mention it." Shirley pulled down the visor and looked into the makeup mirror. Her face was swollen and tear-streaked. "I look hideous. My face always turns blotchy when I cry."

Rita still looked pressed and poised. "That was *some* initiation. I hope you realize I didn't plan to get you involved headfirst like that."

Shirley felt the tears surface again. More like *heart-first*, she thought.

Rita handed her a fresh tissue from her purse. "Would you like me to take you home now?"

"I don't know," said Shirley honestly. "I'm feeling . . ." She searched for the word, but it did not come.

"Give it a while to let things settle," said Rita softly. "You've had a whopping dose of reality today. I remember how affected I was by my first encounter with a women's shelter."

Shirley wadded the tissue and wiped her nose. "Tell me about it."

"I can't," said Rita evenly. There was a distant look in her eyes. "I'm sorry. There are just some things a million dollars worth of therapy can't fix."

Shirley thought she was beginning to understand her new friend better. While Shirley felt sympathy for these people, Rita knew empathy. She wanted to ask Rita about Kathy, she wanted to talk about Stephen, but decided to wait.

"So where are we headed?" she asked instead.

Rita started the car. "Are you sure you're up to another one of my adventures?"

"This is good for me. It really is."

"I've got a delivery to make out to the State Women's Correctional Facility."

"The women's *prison*?"

Rita nodded. "It's one of my most frequent haunts."

"I thought you were new in town."

"I am, but I know the inside of a women's prison. There's not much difference between them no matter where they're located."

Shirley suspected there was so much more to this woman than she was letting show. She checked the time. "I've got two hours before I have to pick up my daughter Sara from preschool."

"Two hours? With any luck and time off for good behavior, I should have you out of maximum security and back home by then."

Six

The only other time Shirley had visited a prison was during a high school field trip. Not much had changed in all those years. Criminals caged in exchange for crimes committed. The dormant psychologist in her still believed there had to be a better way. She'd give it some thought later, after the baby came.

Security was stringent, but no one searched Shirley's belly to see if she was hiding a cake and a file, or maybe a watermelon for the inmates' annual picnic.

"Pretty depressing," Shirley whispered to Rita, who nodded in agreement. The walls, floor, and ceiling were all void and bleak. Cold. Stone-like. So were most of the faces of the women they encountered, but not all of them.

"Hi, Rita," said a woman who Shirley hoped was a security guard, since she was wearing a uniform and carrying a gun. "Good to see you again. I think you really cheered up a couple of the girls last time you were here."

"I hope so, RuthAnn. Another guard is bringing in a couple of boxes of books for the library. I thought you could use them."

"Sure can. Any good romance novels?"

Rita laughed. "It's all fiction—all fantasy."

RuthAnn winked. "That's the way we like it around here."

Rita then made the introductions.

"Are you a guard or the prison matron?" asked Shirley.

RuthAnn grinned. "I guess technically, I'm a guard, but I like to think of myself as a part-time counselor and a former inmate."

Shirley's face could not disguise her surprise.

"That's right, girl. Ever heard of rehabilitation?"

Rita reached over and pushed Shirley's open mouth closed. "She's teasing you, Shirley."

"I knew that," said Shirley, wanting to clarify, Teasing me about which part—being a counselor, a guard, or a reformed inmate?

Again, RuthAnn laughed. "Don't worry. You're as safe in here as you are out on the streets."

That didn't exactly dispel Shirley's anxiety, but it was quieted when the women were led to a small, drab room with a big oak table and unmatched chairs. Two large bookcases held a few dozen tattered books. "Welcome to the library," said RuthAnn. "It's also our counsel room and sometimes our poker-playing hideaway."

The same wave of despair that had washed over her back at the shelter now hit her again, full-force. "I don't think I can do this," confessed Shirley, absorbing the despair that was abundant.

"Sure you can," RuthAnn piped in. "We're all just a gathering of sisters. Harmless as any gathering of ax-murderessess."

Rita grinned and pretended to scold RuthAnn for taking such brutal advantage of Shirley's gullibility.

"You don't have to do anything unless you feel comfortable," assured Rita, "but I do think you're a natural. Remember, I just saw you work wonders with a disheveled little boy."

Three or four other women walked in just then. They weren't inmates, but some sort of employees, who quietly exchanged pleasantries with Rita and RuthAnn about the workings of the prison. Then six women, dressed in identical bright-orange coveralls, entered. There were no handcuffs, no balls-and-chains, but the women were tethered just the same. Invisible leg-irons. Shirley could sense it in the way they shuffled, in tiny careful steps, fearful of making the wrong move. Or perhaps fearful because they had already made the wrong move and didn't wish for any repeats.

Shirley stared at them, one by one, the same way she would have if they had been a lineup of Hollywood superstars—wide-eyed and disbelieving.

The inmates sat down at the table without saying much to anyone, mostly averting their eyes, except for a quick glance in Rita's direction, and a pause or two toward Shirley's stomach.

"Do these women all know you?" Shirley asked her friend.

"No, not really. That's why they are safe with me. I'm sort of a stranger. I only met them a few days ago. But I just do with them what you did with me the other day—I listen."

"You don't give advice?"

"I don't have any to give."

Shirley shifted nervously, aware that she was being recruited. She was self-conscious by nature, but now she felt the eyes of every woman in the room on her, eyeballing her big belly. "I could use some now."

RuthAnn put her arm around Shirley's shoulder and they stepped out into the hallway. "You're not here to save the world, kid. Just to listen. The gals in there are our best-behaved inmates. They've earned the right to be here. Many of these women go weeks, even months without a visitor. All you have to do is introduce yourself and then give them a chance to talk. The women in this program have all requested a visitor, so your work is a piece of cake."

When Shirley finally agreed to try, RuthAnn advised her of the rules.

Walk away if you feel too uncomfortable with what is being said.

Do not divulge more about yourself than you want to.

Don't make promises, loan money, etc.

There were several dos and don'ts. They were common sense rules, and Shirley understood their necessity.

"The woman you'll be visiting is named Lou. Are you a good judge of character?"

Shirley lifted her shoulders. "I guess. Why?"

RuthAnn grinned. "Because, girl, Lou is some character!"

When Shirley re-entered the room, all of the women were engaged in hushed conversation except one woman who sat at the end of the table waiting. Shirley guessed her to be about sixty. The lines of life were etched deeply in her face. Her gray-streaked hair was slicked back into a pony tail and fastened with a rubber band. She must have sensed Shirley's hesitation because she immediately stood and held out her hand.

"Hi, I'm Lou."

Shirley took her hand and sat next to her. "I'm Shirley," she said softly.

"You've never been in the joint before." It wasn't a question. "Oh, don't worry. None of us are here for doing another bodily harm, at least not with intent." She laughed at her own joke, but Shirley couldn't even manage a smile.

"I'm sorry for being so apprehensive," said Shirley.

"Don't worry about it," said Lou, curving her upper lip to reveal a missing front tooth. "We're just glad people like you show up at all. And it's not very often that we get a volunteer visitor who is about to have a kid. You look like you're about to burst. When are you due—two days?"

"A little over two weeks."

Lou tried to whistle, but blew mostly silent air through her lips. "You must be miserable."

"To say the least."

"That kid kickin' away at your bladder?"

Shirley smiled. "You must be a mother." The thought made Shirley freeze.

"Most of us in here are mothers."

That piece of information took a moment to register. Today was turning out to be a crash course in Life 101.

"This time of year must be difficult for you." She had picked up that sentiment from Pat earlier in the day.

Lou's face showed no emotion. "I guess it is. I always hated Mother's Day anyway. But I love kids and I'm glad to see women bringing new life to this old world."

Shirley was amazed at Lou's straightforwardness and positive attitude.

"Tell me about yourself," Shirley invited awkwardly.

"You want to know what I'm in for."

"Am I that transparent?"

"It's the first question on everyone's mind. I'm here for armed robbery. I held up the dance studio where my little granddaughter used to take ballet lessons."

Lou just sat there while Shirley's eyes begged for details. "Did they do something to offend you?"

That made Lou laugh out loud, and all of the other women in the room turned to see what was so funny.

"Offend me? Oh, no. The dance people didn't offend me. My son-in-law offended me. You see, my daughter is in prison in Oklahoma, doing life for killing that monster. She caught him raping their daughter. She stabbed him in the back with a kitchen knife. Oklahoma put her away and I got little Shannon.

"To make a long story short, I couldn't offer Shannon much better, so I figured if I got some money, we'd make a clean start. I knew them dance people had a wad of money on Friday nights, so I held 'em up and got away with more than two thousand bucks."

Shirley's hand covered her mouth, a gesture of shock at Lou's tale.

"Turns out old Grandma wasn't much of a thief. Don't got the brains. We got as far as Chicago before they had me locked up."

Shirley wondered for a moment if Lou wasn't making all of this up just because Shirley was new and had already proven her gullibility. "What happened to Shannon?" she asked.

"The state of Illinois has her. At least, they had her for six years. She's eighteen now and living not far from Oklahoma City. She sees her mother regularly. I get a letter once in a while and we're trying to work it out so she can come visit me this summer if I make parole."

As the minutes ticked away, Shirley was convinced that Lou was telling the truth. The terrible truth. She talked so fast, spit flew in every direction, but the woman obviously felt a need to talk, and knew she had to talk fast. She told one story after another, each about her life as a woman of not-so-quiet desperation. She had served a stint in the navy as a WAC, worked as a 911 operator, and sold used vacuum cleaners. She'd had enough men to call herself a pro, but had never taken money for her generosity. She had one daughter and one granddaughter. When she got out of "the joint," she intended to hook up with a job that would ultimately take her to Oklahoma.

"I like animals," she said. "Big animals. Horses, mainly. I guess they got plenty of horses in Oklahoma. I'll get a horse job down there so I can be near my girls."

Shirley listened, enthralled by Lou's storytelling abilities. Shirley didn't have to worry about any of the prison rules being violated. Lou knew them all and kept within the boundaries. She just wanted to talk and loved having a new audience. The stories continued for twenty minutes until Rita announced it was time to go.

Shirley reached out and touched Lou's leathered cheek. "Would you mind if I come again?"

"That'd be nice. But wait until after you have the kid.

Then both of you come by and see us, and we can see both of you!"

Shirley promised she would.

The ride back to Shirley's house was relatively quiet. She felt like she'd been to another planet and was having a difficult time assimilating the whole experience.

"I hope you don't mind leaving your comfort zone like that," said Rita.

Shirley thought for a minute before responding. "I probably did at first. I've always been content to stay at home where the most dangerous aspect of my life is the dog when she's in heat. This was good for me today. Really good for me."

"I think you have a natural gift to lift people."

"Thanks, but I was thinking that same thing about you. How long have you been a rescuing angel, Rita?"

Rita looked at her uneasily. "I'm no angel and I don't do much rescuing, but I do spend at least one day a week out with the people whom our foundations benefit. Actually, I enjoy the rounds more than just about any other aspect of my job."

"Well, people sure seem to think the world of you."

"You know, it's funny—I just moved from one city to another. It doesn't matter how many state lines there are between shelters, the places are the same. The faces are the same. The prison is almost identical to the one where I'd worked before."

"What do you think will happen to Kathy and Stephen?" asked Shirley, her mind unable to forget them, even for a moment.

"I'm really not sure. Kathy was beginning to open up and talk when we left. Dr. Memford is the psychologist working with her. He is supposed to be great. I know Pat will give her all the support she can, too. I think what really helped was when you got Stephen to open up. If anyone can get through to Kathy, it will be her son. You really did work a miracle with that little boy, Shirley."

"I think it was the other way around. Do you think Kathy will go back to her husband?"

"Probably. I know Dr. Memford has been doing some grief counseling with him as well. The aim here is to put the family back together if that's what's best," Rita said.

"How do you know what's best?"

"You don't always."

The mood was getting a little heavy and Shirley was feeling the weight.

"What did you think of Lou?" Shirley asked.

"She's something else. Maybe because her wounds are not as fresh as Kathy's, but that woman has been injured. A scarred soul with an incredible attitude. She'll probably end up working with horses in Oklahoma, as long as that's what she really wants."

"She was so engaging," Shirley said.

"If only you could get her to overcome her shyness and talk about herself," Rita joked.

Shirley smiled. "How do you know so much about Lou?"

"I spent a session with her last week."

"Wow," said Shirley. "I learned more about the intimate details of her life in twenty minutes than I'll learn about my husband's in twenty years."

Shirley made it safely back into her "comfort zone" just in time to pick up Sara from preschool. She had forgotten that Samantha and Sean had afternoon dental appointments. So it was back to the elementary and then to the junior high school. While the dentist was examining them, Shirley sat on the couch in the waiting room, cuddled with Sara.

"Will you please read me *Koala Lou?*" Sara asked, reaching for her mother's purse.

"It's not in there," said Shirley. "Mama gave it away."

Sara's eyes narrowed. "You gave my *Koala Lou* away?"

Shirley kissed her forehead. "Yes, baby. Mama gave your storybook away—to a little boy who really needed to hear that some stories *do* have happy endings."

Seven

All that night and into the next day, Shirley wondered about Kathy, Pat, Lou and every other woman with whom she had come in contact at the shelter and the prison. Were they safe? Warm? Was Kathy talking yet? Was anyone listening to Lou? Most of all, Shirley wondered about Stephen. Who was reading to him? Who was holding him? Maybe she should go back there and bring him home. No. That would not be right, probably not even legal.

The image of that child Stephen—his wide, searching eyes, his unsteady voice, his desperate touch, even his lonely smell, all permeated Shirley's thoughts, haunting her with every blink.

Shirley shared her experiences and feelings with Stan.

"Don't you wonder what all of those people did before yesterday when you were first introduced into their lives?"

Her emotions were on the brink, a cacophony of feelings expanding without ever contracting. "Don't make fun of this," she warned him. "You don't have a clue what it was like. What *they* were like. I knew this world was full of people in pain, but . . ."

Stan smiled understandingly, reached out and stroked the curve of her jaw with the back of his fingers. "I thought you were joking when you told us that you'd spent the day in prison."

Shirley tried to smile, but couldn't. "I feel so overwhelmed. So inadequate. The need is so endless. I know Rita does public relations work for foundations that support places like the women's shelter. She makes a difference. That's all it takes, people willing to get in and actually *do* something, and not just *feel bad*."

"You don't have to convince *me*," said Stan. "It sounds like Rita's made it her life's work, but what can people like us do to help?"

"I'm not sure," she admitted. Then she grinned.

"Oh, no," said Stan. "That's the grin that reminds me of a tornado warning. I know something's coming and I had best just step out of the way."

Shirley headed into the family room, where Samantha was in front of the television. "Come on, Sami," said Shirley. "Let's go."

Samantha stood up. "Where are we going? To the mall? I need some pink fingernail polish and a new bra. Let's go."

"I've got a much more educational experience in mind," Shirley said, ripping a page from the telephone book.

They spent the next hour driving around looking for the local homeless shelter, not the women's shelter, the more generic homeless shelter that was open to the public. Maybe it just seemed like an hour to Shirley because her teenage daughter kept whining, "Why the homeless shelter, Mom? We don't know anyone there."

"That's the whole point. We're reaching out past our comfort zones."

"I'm comfortable at the mall, Mom. And besides, there are plenty of homeless people at the mall if you're looking for someone to talk to."

Shirley sighed. She wasn't getting through to her daughter. "The world is a bigger place than just our house, the mall, and your school. I simply want us to help people who are not as blessed as we are."

"You're trying to copy your friend Rita."
"I am not," Shirley denied a little too adamantly.

"That's it!" said Shirley, pulling the car against the curb.
"*That's* the homeless shelter?" asked Samantha, pointing to a red brick building with a big cement porch. "It looks like an old house."

"It probably is," said Shirley, sliding carefully out of the car sideways, because the baby had shifted low and fit snugly against the bottom curve of the steering wheel, even with the driver's seat pushed back as far as it would go. She wasn't about to get herself stuck again with only Sami to rescue her.

"How come there are no signs or anything?"

Shirley squinted, surveying the brick building and neglected yard. "I don't know. Maybe for privacy. But this is the address in the phone book."

Samantha followed her mother reluctantly, but Shirley approached the front door with all of the energy and confidence she could muster after walking up fourteen steps. She laced her fingers, cradled the bottom of her belly and lifted once or twice. The baby was riding lower by the minute. She hoped the homeless shelter had a public rest room.

"Don't be so nervous," she instructed Samantha. "Yesterday I about hyperventilated when I first walked in to the women's shelter. Don't worry. No one here is going to hurt us."

Samantha tucked her head until her chin touched her chest. She was holding her own wrists behind her back and looked, to Shirley, more like a would-be resident than a would-be volunteer.

Shirley moved a pile of dry dead leaves with the side of her shoe. The smell of rotting leaves, damp dirt, and sour garbage forced Shirley's hand to her mouth before she was able to reach up and rap five hard times on the big weathered wooden door.

No answer.

No doorbell.

"There could be crazy people in there," said Samantha, reaching forward, squeezing her mother's hand. "Whatever happened to all the years of 'Never talk to strangers'?"

"You pick *now* to start listening to me?" She knocked again.

There was still no answer and Samantha tugged on Shirley's sleeve. This time Shirley reached out and tried the knob. The door was locked.

"That's so odd. The place can't be empty in the middle of the day."

Now Samantha was really beginning to panic. "Mom, let's go! This is creepy. I'm going back to the car."

Shirley drove to the nearest gas station, used the rest room, bought Samantha a bottled drink to pacify her and then returned to the front of the homeless shelter. Still no sign of life.

They were sitting in the car trying to decide what to do when Samantha said, "Look, Mom!"

There was a woman with two small children crossing the street and heading directly for the shelter.

"Doesn't she look tired?" asked Shirley. "Look at that poor woman, she's slouching. Her hair probably hasn't been washed in weeks, and her clothes are not much more than rags. And her children . . . they are just as unkempt and needy." Shirley reached for the handle of the car door.

"Don't you dare, Mom! Please! The woman doesn't need to be attacked by strangers."

"Okay," relented Shirley, "but let's make sure they get in the shelter before we leave. If they are locked out, then we'll volunteer to help them now, okay?"

"Okay."

"If they make it inside, we'll go home and I'll call the

shelter's number to make sure they are all right and see if there is anything we can do for them."

Samantha was so relieved she volunteered, "I've got some old clothes and toys those kids are welcome to have."

"Now you're getting into the spirit of this whole thing," Shirley said, reaching to touch Samantha's hand.

They continued to watch as the woman and her children seemed to have no trouble at all entering the building.

"The poor waifs," said Shirley.

All the way home she thought of ways she wanted to help that poor woman and her children. She imagined a terror of tales behind their plight to the shelter. The minute she got home, Shirley went right for the telephone.

A woman answered on the second ring.

"Hello, I was down at your shelter a little while ago. No one was there in the middle of the day."

"That's because we close the shelter at certain times during the day to encourage our people to go out and look for work."

"What about lunch?" Shirley asked

"This shelter only provides breakfast and dinner and a warm place to stay. It's not a permanent residence or a free hotel."

The woman's curtness caught Shirley off guard. "Well, while we were there, we saw a poor woman and her two small children enter your shelter," Shirley explained rapidly. "The poor mother looked ancient and haggard. Terrible. The kids, too, a boy and a girl about three and four. I could tell they were destitute. Ragged. Dirty. Probably starving. They looked so pathetic, I just had to call and volunteer my services.

Shirley was now short of breath, but had to continue before she lost her nerve. "I have a degree in psychology and I'm very astute. I have to admit I have terrific people skills."

The woman did not reply for a very long time. When she did, her words were weighed and delivered very cautiously. "I am the manager of this shelter. Those dirty, ragged, pathetic children are mine. When you saw us, we were just returning from lunch down the street. This is how we look every day. Thanks a lot, lady, but I don't think we'll be needing *your* people skills."

Click.

The rest of the afternoon dragged on and on for Shirley. "I feel like such an idiot," she confessed to Stan.

"Your heart was in the right place." He tried to make her feel better, but the truth was, he found the whole thing so comical, he could not quit laughing. "Did you really call her kids pathetic?" He broke up again.

"Be quiet and go call your grandma to make sure she got the flowers for Mother's Day. Call mine while you're at it."

He continued laughing.

"And go visit your mother. Tell her I said happy Mother's Day. Her gift certificate and card are in the kitchen drawer. Then take Sara to chorus rehearsal and Sean to get his hair cut."

Stan kept chuckling while Shirley gave orders. "How about your mom, doesn't she usually stop by and collect her Mother's Day gift in person?" he asked.

"She already has, so you don't have to drive all the way to her house." Shirley went over to the dresser and picked up a package. "Look what Mom brought me for Mother's Day."

The package contained a book entitled *Lose the Baby Fat Before the Kid Is in Kindergarten* and a five-pound tub of pecan fudge.

"You keep the book," said Stan. "I think she meant the fudge for me." He reached out to take it from her.

"One inch closer and you won't be able to count past seven because you'll be missing three fingers!"

"Come on, kids!" he yelled. "We're going to the mall!"

Eight

Shirley couldn't sleep that night. It wasn't just the humiliation, the baby was giving in to gravity and Shirley felt like its head had dropped down to her knees. Where does that leave the rest of my innards? she thought.

She also lay awake fretting about Mother's Day, which was only a few hours away. All the flowers had been delivered. She had talked to both mothers and both grandmothers. The other tokens of affection had also been parceled out to adoptive mothers and teachers and neighbors.

Their family sure had a lot to be thankful for, she realized, lying there in the darkness. It was filled with people who cared about them. Shirley had already received cards and telephone calls and even some gifts from women who wanted to honor her as a mother as well. The only one who didn't say as much as "Happy Mother's Day" was her mother-in-law. But that was typical, and Shirley didn't let it bother her. She vowed that when her children had families of their own, Shirley would be the first to honor her daughters and daughters-in-law on Mother's Day. She would not sit around and wait for them to remember her.

Then she laughed at her own insightfulness; after all, everyone now knew what an *astute* people person she was.

Because of her recent experiences with Rita, Shirley did

know that her view of Mother's Day would remain forever changed.

When she was a young girl, she had loved making clay ashtrays and beaded necklaces for her own mother. There was even a very special messy drawer where Lena put them "for safekeeping." Shirley never saw her mother actually wear one of the necklaces or use one of the ashtrays. It had never dawned on Shirley that Lena didn't smoke; she could have used them for candy dishes, or just sat them out to be admired among the many knickknacks that adorned their home. But no, they were kept safe and hidden in a special drawer.

As a teenager, Shirley dreamed of the day her own husband and children would bear her gifts and make her queen for a day.

As an actual mother, Shirley grew to hate the holiday. She felt guilty for not remotely resembling anything that the cards described. She was not the loving, patient counselor and enthusiastic seamstress and chef that Hallmark paid homage to.

Now, lying awake with the moonlight streaming through the drapes, Shirley's mind focused on motherhood in a way that it never had before. While she whined to her family and friends about the drudgery of homemaking, there were women who had no homes. There were mothers who were deprived of their own children. She thought of Pat. Shirley had been shocked to learn from Rita that the reason Pat was at the shelter was because she had once come through those doors in need of a safe place.

Rita wasn't sure of the details, but she knew that Pat had lost custody of her children and never got them back. They were adults now, and Shirley couldn't help but wonder if Pat would hear from them this weekend.

She thought of Lou and of three generations of women in that family. She wondered how they would remember each other on Mother's Day.

She thought of Rita. What was *her* story, and when would their friendship be secure enough so that Rita would really open up?

Most of all, Shirley concentrated on Kathy and Stephen. She hated to think what Mother's Day would be like for Kathy this year. Maybe God would be merciful and make her numb, even oblivious to what was going on around her for that day.

When Shirley realized that she was not going to be able to sleep, she managed to get herself to the adjoining bathroom and decided to soak in a bed of bubbles. All she could find were Sara's clown ones, but they worked, and Shirley emptied the bottle into a steaming stream of water. Actually, it didn't take much, because as soon as Shirley climbed into the tub, the water level rose to the top.

She lay back, relaxing as best she could and feeling very, very appreciative for this kicking gymnast in her belly. She thanked God for those three other sleeping children and for the man who had made this life possible for her.

Quietly, she yawned and began to doze.

"Stan!" she shouted. "Wake up!"

She heard the bedsprings squeak as he rolled over. "Where are you?"

"In here," she croaked.

"Where?"

"I'm in the bathtub."

Stan stumbled into the bathroom. "Are you stuck in there?"

"Not yet."

"What are you doing?"

"Soaking."

"Is everything okay?"

"Yes. Would you care to join me?" she joked.

He looked at her. "You remind me of that twenty-pound

turkey you tried to stuff into a ten-pound roaster. Remember?"

It was a vicious comment, but it was the middle of the night and her pale, cellulite-ridden body did overflow the tub. Yes, she had to admit the comparison was not far from accurate.

"Would you do me a favor?" she asked.

Stan was still too sleepy to realize just what he was in for. "I guess."

"Would you shave my legs?" she asked.

By sunrise, Shirley was feeling almost emancipated. Removing three months' worth of leg hair does that to a woman. She had to admit that Stan had been a great sport. So what if he did dull six disposables; he saw it to the end.

"Next time I'm ragging on you," she said, "remind me of this night. That's about the sexiest thing you ever did. You really are a woman's man, Stanley."

"No, I'm not. I'm a manly man and I'm going back to bed."

After doing her hair and makeup, Shirley carefully lay back down by him, thinking she'd just close her eyes and rest for a minute. She had such a great jump on this highest holy day of days. . . .

"Wake up, Mommy!"

"Happy Mother's Day."

"I made you breakfast."

"No, you didn't! Dad made the eggs. Sara made the toast. I made the juice. You didn't do anything!"

"Did so! It was my idea!"

"Jerk!"

Stan cleared his throat. "Shirley, it's going to be a wonderful day. Rise and shine!"

Shirley opened one eye. There they were. The whole

family, grinning like morons and holding out offerings that looked like recycled science projects.

She put the pillow over her face, but someone pulled it off.

"Wake up, Mom. It's Mother's Day."

Not only had Shirley fallen back to sleep, she'd entered into one of those deep REM sleeps that her mother used to refer to as Darvon dreams. Someone pulled her forward and she wiped her face with the back of her hand.

"Is that drool?" asked Samantha with disgust.

After that, no one wanted to kiss her. But Samantha did hand her a plate of eggs and toast. A faded plastic rose lay artistically across the top.

"Thanks, sweetheart. It looks delicious."

"We made breakfast," said Sean. "Samantha burned the bacon."

"Did not! If it was so burned, why did you pig it all?"

"Don't fight, you two," said Stan. "This is Mother's Day. No contention on Mother's Day."

Sean handed Shirley a piece of foil-covered cardboard with a million Popsicle sticks protruding from various directions. "Sean! This is your space station project."

"I want you to have it." He stepped forward and almost kissed her, but then coiled back quickly. "I forgot about the drool," he explained.

Shirley wiped her mouth with a single sheet of paper towel that accompanied her breakfast meal.

Next came Sara. "Surprise!"

She handed Shirley a . . .

"Do you like it, Mommy? It's my surprise from pre-school." Her little eyes pleaded for praise.

"Mommy loves it," she said. "It's beautiful." Shirley's eyes searched Stan's, then Samantha's, and then Sean's for help, but they were all looking downward.

Then Sara asked the question that makes every mother squirm. "Do you know what it is?"

Shirley felt like a fly caught between a ravenous spider and a new sticky piece of flypaper. Either way, she was a goner. She hesitated just long enough to make Sara's brow furrow and her bottom lip pout.

"You can't even tell what it is, can you?"

"Sure I can." The rest of the family still wouldn't look at her to help.

"What is it then?"

"It's a . . . it's a . . . a paperweight!"

Wrong! The look on little Sara's face was heartbreaking.

"It's a bottle holder for the new baby," she informed everyone. "I made it all by myself."

"And you did a marvelous job," said Shirley. "I'm so silly. It looks just like a bottle holder. Mommy's still sleepy."

Shirley then looked to Stan. So did the kids. It was his turn.

"Um, um . . . I don't have your present here," he stuttered. "Besides, you're not my mother."

He was joking, and Shirley knew he was—or he'd be a dead man.

"Dinner's at six at the bistro," he announced. "Now eat breakfast before it gets cold."

Shirley was on her second slice of toast when she finally awoke fully. "What time is it now?" she asked.

"It's nine-twenty," Stan answered.

"Oh, no!" Shirley screamed. "Church starts at ten and nobody's ready!"

Nine

Shirley barked orders and had the kids jumping to command like only a mother in motion can. Then she went into the bathroom to do what damage repair she could on her face and hair. She had looked better with no sleep than she did now with her face puffy, her hair smashed, and her makeup caked, ground in, and smeared from ear to ear.

She did what she could and then slipped her only nice maternity dress over her head. "Now my hair is ruined again," she complained aloud. She had never felt so fat and unattractive in her entire life. Her emotions were in charge today.

They always were on Mother's Day.

"You're going to leave me, aren't you?" she asked Stan when he came into the room.

"I am if you don't hurry," he said, buttoning his long-sleeved white shirt. She was grateful she had sent it out to be laundered. At least it looked clean and pressed.

"Samantha says she needs to get there early because she's giving a tribute to you, and the pastor asked her to sit on the stand with the other speakers."

"I'm almost ready," Shirley said, locking herself in the bathroom. Getting her panty hose on required more time and energy than everything else combined. It also required strict privacy. It was such a degrading procedure, she didn't want even those closest to her to witness the event.

First she wadded them up and put her toes in, then she began the ridiculous ritual of pulling, tugging, and shifting. During her first pregnancy, her gynecologist, a portly man, *then* past the age of retirement, shared a secret with Shirley for which she would be forever grateful. "If you cut a straight line from the top of your panty hose waistband down to just before the crotch, the material won't run, but it will allow a wonderful hole for your belly to breathe and roam free from confinement. And your panty hose actually stay up, none of this down-around-your-knees stuff. That's so uncomfortable."

Shirley's big belly was in need of a little fresh air and roaming space. She could still picture the good doctor with his hands on his own round stomach, explaining the process like one with firsthand experience.

Years later when Shirley heard rumors that the man was a bona fide cross-dresser, she just kept quiet and smiled.

"You look nice," Stan said when Shirley emerged from the bathroom.

"What's that supposed to mean?"

"It means you look nice."

"You're just saying that because it's Mother's Day," Shirley said.

"No. I'm not."

"I look fat."

"You're pregnant."

"So you're saying I look fat."

"No."

"Then *what* are you saying?"

"Just that you're pregnant," Stan told her.

"Oh, so I'm fat *and* pregnant!"

"No—just pregnant."

"Pregnant women look bloated. Do I look bloated?"

"No."

"Pregnant women look tired. Do I look tired?" Shirley asked.

"No."

"Pregnant women look miserable. Do I look miserable?"

"Not at all."

"Liar!"

"Samantha, do you have your talk ready?" Shirley asked. "You know, you really should have let me hear it first."

"Not a chance, Mom."

"Sean, let me check your suit. You look so handsome. I like your haircut."

"Thanks. Is that all?"

"Just remember to—"

"I know, I know. Don't take my jacket off, or people will know you didn't iron *my* shirt. Make sure every woman in the congregation gets a flower and not just the women who have had babies. Be polite. Sit up straight. Don't mess around with the other boys, and keep my fingers out of my nose."

"I've trained you well, my son."

"Sara, do you remember the words to your songs? If you forget, just move your mouth."

"Where's your necklace, Mommy?"

"What necklace?"

Sara's shoulders drooped. "The one I made you last Mother's Day. You said you'd wear it every Mother's Day for the rest of your life. You promised."

"How do you remember what I said last year?"

"Dad reminded me."

Shirley went to her jewelry box and fished out a macaroni necklace. At least it wasn't hidden away in some special drawer, although it was missing a few shells, and the fishing line showed all the way around. She slipped it on over her head. So much for her hair, she thought, plotting Father's Day revenge against her devoted husband. She'd make sure he wore the tie Sean made from refuse on Save the World Day. The tie actually had pieces of garbage glued to it!

"Stan! You're still not ready. We've got to go—now!"

He stood in the doorway, not looking at her. "I'm not going with you."

"What?"

"I just got a call from the office. I've got to go in and send a fax off to Japan."

She could tell from the look on his face that he was not kidding. "It's Mother's Day. Japanese people have mothers. Tell them you'll do it first thing in the morning," she practically begged.

"I would, Shirley, but I can't. It's my lousy boss, Curtis—he's the guy who never had a mother."

Shirley flopped back onto the bed. "You *have* to to church go with me," she moaned.

"I can't."

"But I can't waddle in there with all these kids."

"Why not? You do it every week."

"Sometimes you come with us."

"You say I'm not any help even when I do come with you. You say you do everything by yourself anyway."

"Fine. Fine. Just go then. Happy Mother's Day to me!"

"Lighten up. I'll be here when you get home—and remember we're on for dinner tonight."

The ride to church was *not* pleasant. Every inch of Shirley was ornery and miserable. She did her best not to take it out on the children, who were huddled together in the backseat, acting like they had to protect each other from their own mother.

"I'm not that wretched, am I?"

No one responded.

"Well, don't worry. Homo sapiens don't eat their young." Shirley attempted to lighten the mood with humor. It didn't work.

"This is your dad's fault, I hope you know. If he was here, I'd be in a good mood."

Still no comment from the backseat.

"I'm sorry," Shirley whispered to each child as they emerged from the car. "I love you. I'm just having a bad morning."

"Are you in another bad mood or is it the same one as always?" asked Sean.

Shirley felt the guilt sweep over her like a solar eclipse, drowning out even the faintest trace of light from her world.

"Just call this my Mother's Day mood," she answered, knowing full well that if her children were not participating in the church program, she would be home in bed with the covers pulled way over her head. There she would stay for the next two weeks until the baby was born.

"What's wrong, Mommy?" Sara asked, slipping her trusting hand in her mother's.

Shirley almost said "everything," but caught herself, and answered, "Nothing. Mommy is fine."

Really, she was. Shirley knew that in comparison to some other women, she had nothing to complain about. Nothing at all. That only brought on more guilt and made her feel even worse.

"Good morning, Shirley!" a chipper voice called from the car just pulling up next to theirs. It was Mertyl Casper and her triplets. They were really spaced two years apart, but Mertyl was one of those women who not only sewed, she actually owned a serger and wasn't afraid to use it. Her daughters, ages twelve, ten and eight, were always decked in triplicate. Matching floral frills. Shirley could see that today's pattern was pink petunias or some such flower. The girls had matching bonnets, gloves, and unscuffed white shoes.

"I know it's not Memorial Day yet," apologized Mertyl when she saw Shirley eyeing her daughters' feet, "but I didn't think it would hurt to fudge when it's so close, do you?"

Shirley guessed she was referring to some stupid etiquette rule about not wearing white shoes too early in the fashion season. "No, I think it's okay to fudge—just this *once*, Mertyl."

Sara was wearing her Easter dress, the one Sean had ripped the bow off of. Shirley had stapled it on just as they were going out the door, but now it hung funny and the staple was showing.

"Stand behind somebody," Shirley instructed, ushering Sara into the building. Sean and Samantha had run ahead the minute Mertyl Casper had pulled into the parking lot. The oldest Casper girl had a crush on Sean, and he wanted to get as far away from her as possible.

I don't know why I let people like her get to me, thought Shirley, but I do. Mother's Day was created to honor people like Mertyl Casper, not women like me.

It was almost time for the service to begin and Shirley thought she was safe.

Not so.

"I see you haven't had that baby *yet*," said Brother Hopkins, an old bachelor who used to coach football.

"Not yet," said Shirley.

"I bet he'll weigh enough to play quarterback when he is finally born."

"I'm feeling that way."

Someone else patted Shirley's stomach. "We're all betting on twins," said a well-meaning elderly sister.

"Don't count me in on that bet," said Shirley.

A few more pats and remarks of astonishment about her size, and Shirley made it into the chapel. "Make way for Shirley," said the pastor. He took her by the hand. "Welcome, and happy Mother's Day. I see that Stan is not with you."

"No, he's not." She offered no excuses.

"Please have a seat. We're looking forward to Samantha's remarks."

"Thanks. I am, too."

By the time Shirley had squeezed into a seat in the third row, she had overheard another barrage of remarks about her size, most of them meant to be whispers, but the acoustics in the place were remarkable.

Brother McMurrary, blind as a bat, patted Shirley's fanny. "My goodness, but that baby is taking up a lot of space," he said loud enough for everyone to hear.

Shirley suspected that the man was not so impaired that he could not distinguish front from rear, but she had no way of proving the geezer was a pervert.

The first congregational hymn was underway before Shirley looked up and around. She saw Samantha sitting on the stand along with Mertyl Casper's middle daughter, the one with bright-red ringlets tied with giant pink bows.

Pink and red clash, thought Shirley nastily. Then she noticed that Samantha was wearing hammered gym shoes with her Sunday velvet.

Sean was sitting in the corner in the front row with the other boys in his Sunday-school class. They were all wearing suits and sporting new haircuts. They all looked a little nervous, waiting for the pastor to announce that it was time for the flower brigade.

Sara sat next to Shirley, singing confidently at the top of her lungs. Never mind that she was off key or that she didn't know the words. The little girl was singing with the confidence of Streisand, and that's what mattered to her mother.

Why had Shirley been such a beast this morning? As soon as the pastor began his traditional sermon on motherhood, Shirley remembered. She sank a little lower, the guilt riding on her shoulders. She purposely did her best to drown out his praises. She began looking at the people with whom she had gone to church most of her married life.

There sat Jennifer, holding a two-month-old baby. Shirley had hosted her shower. Jennifer was just sixteen, on her own and determined to raise her daughter by herself. Shirley admired her spirit, but didn't envy her road ahead.

In front of Jennifer was Peggy. Peggy had never given birth, but was as motherly as a woman could get. She did adopt two children from somewhere in Central or South America. They were grown now and lived out of town. Still, Peggy's lap always had a child on it. She was the grandmother of the congregation, and you had to book her months in advance if you wanted her to baby-sit on a weekend. Today was for her.

In the next pew over sat widow Woodard. That woman had raised seven sons, after being widowed while pregnant with the seventh. She had also managed to go back to college and earn her teaching certificate. Now, *she* was a mother.

Julie sat behind Shirley. Julie and her husband had been married for nine years. For eight of those years they had been trying to conceive a child with "no luck." Julie liked to joke that luck had nothing to do with it. It was timing and temperature and the number of swimming lessons a sperm had had. She was always making jokes, but Shirley wondered about her feelings today.

Sister Smith sat on the stand. She lead the children's chorus. She had a children's chorus of her own, too. The woman's body had actually given birth to eleven children! Eleven! Yet, there she sat, legs crossed, looking like a college coed. It was a medical mystery. Of course she claimed it was diet and exercise, but Shirley suspected the woman had some miracle pill that dissolved fat and cellulite. That didn't explain her perky attitude and abundant energy. Shirley also thought her hair looked a little too shiny and her husband a little too smiley. Shirley wanted to hate the woman, but she couldn't. Sister Smith was one of the nicest, most genuine women Shirley had ever known. And the woman was totally devoted to her family. Mother's Day was for women like Sister Smith.

Shirley saw the women that were there, but she also saw the faces that were *not* present. Angela wasn't there. She was at the hospital with her son Jamal, who had been hit by a car on New Year's Day. Today was to celebrate devotion like Angela's.

Betty was not there. She had miscarried a few months ago, and had told Shirley that she didn't feel much like coming to church on Mother's Day.

Neither Betsy or Jessica were there. Neither one of them had ever had children. Betsy had never married; Jessica was married, but opted not to have children. Last year on Mother's Day, the women had told Shirley they were going to get together every Mother's Day and celebrate with dinner and videos. Away from families and children.

Mother's Day would never be the same for Shirley. The idea behind it was okay, but it still caused a lot of unintentional pain for women, depending on their lives. I've really been trapped in a narrow world, thought Shirley, wondering about the shelter, the prison. What were those women doing at this moment?

Shirley shifted uncomfortably. Her bladder was full again, but she couldn't leave now and risk missing her children's contributions to the services. The pastor was saying something about the demise of the American family. As of

1980 only fourteen percent of American homes were composed of the traditional father, mother, and children.

1980? What about today?

Shirley continued studying faces and silently telling life stories. Statistics were right. More than half of the women in the congregation had been divorced at least once. Shirley was in the minority and she felt like an exception.

The pastor then began talking about the stages of motherhood. There were mothers of infants, toddlers, school-age children, teenagers, young adults, and then there were grandmothers. The thought suddenly occurred to Shirley that she fit four of those categories at once! I should have just had quadruplets and been done with it, she thought.

Someone tapped her on the shoulder. It was Roger Wiltham, Stan's friend.

"Where's the man?" he whispered.

"He had to work for a while today."

"Too bad," said Roger.

Shirley agreed. She wished Stan was sitting beside her now. She was feeling an overpowering need to punch someone.

The pastor attracted Shirley's attention when he began talking about a woman named Anna Jarvis. Apparently she was the one to blame, or thank, for setting aside the second Sunday of every May to honor mothers. She had had predecessors who wanted a day dedicated for peace.

Shirley had to smile at that when she thought about the peace that Mother's Day brought to her household.

Flowers had also been part of the original Mother's Day deal. Carnations were worn by the first women. Colored carnations if the person's mother was living, white if she was deceased. Shirley noted there were only a few carnations in the congregation. She liked the idea of a little living flower, and was glad Sean got to help pass them out this year. She hoped the experience would make him a little

In My Quest for Personal Growth . . .

more appreciative of the women who mothered the world. Probably not, but she could dream.

Mother's Day had been official since 1915 when President Woodrow Wilson was authorized to make it a national observance. What Shirley hoped now was that the pastor observed the clock. If he didn't, there would be a puddle to pay.

When he finally finished, Samantha stood up to the pulpit and looked down at her mother. All she had to do was make eye contact and Shirley started to cry. Here was her firstborn child. Now a teenager. Every un-motherly act she had ever committed came pounding down on Shirley's head.

She was wrought with a million emotions and they were all swarming over her like bees. She just wanted to get out and shake herself free, but she couldn't.

"My mother is the greatest mother in the world," Samantha began.

The kid knew right where to strike and had the perfect weapon—guilt.

Samantha continued that attack. "She's bright, funny, talented, and patient. She is always there for us when we need her. She works at home to help pay the bills. She cleans and cooks all day, too."

As Samantha kept piling it high, Shirley felt buried. She wondered how long it would be before people noticed the smell.

Samantha just continued to drone on and on. Men were now smiling at Shirley. Women were either glaring or avoiding eye contact altogether. It wasn't like Shirley had really betrayed anyone, Samantha was just making it sound like she was a traitor. Shirley wanted to stand up and deny every kind word that her daughter was saying about her. Instead, she died of embarrassment at Samantha's conclusion.

"My mother is always so willing to help us. She helps me with my school reports. She does my tough math homework. She even wrote this Mother's Day talk for me!"

Laughter rippled through the congregation. Shirley

smiled at the joke and then whispered to Sara, "Mommy will be right back. I'm going to the potty."

"I want to come to," Sara stated firmly.

"You have to stay here in case it's your turn to sing."

"Then you'll miss my song. Wait."

"Mommy can't wait, honey."

"Please wait."

"I have to go NOW!" she said a lot louder than she had intended. People stood to clear the way for her to pass.

Ten

Shirley had never felt so conspicuous as she did wriggling out of her own pew and then waddling past row after row, all filled with Sunday-best smiles and nods. Stares that focused on her midsection. I know what they're really thinking, she judged. I know they are all longing for the days when pregnant women were cloistered away.

When Shirley finally made it to the women's rest room, the narrow stalls brought flashbacks of the mall's revolving doors. She wondered how Rita was celebrating the day, and hoped she would decide to join them for dinner later that night.

She left the door ajar while conducting business, but made it out okay, although getting the panty hose back up was one of life's not-so-quiet little miracles. Shirley looked into the long and narrow mirror above the sink while she washed her hands. I really don't look so bad from the neck up, she thought, summoning the courage to go back into the chapel.

Shirley toddled back just in time. Sara was joining the other children in the chorus getting ready to pay homage to mothers through music. Shirley hurried her fastest to the front of the chapel where her own seat was waiting. She noticed people smiling—even brighter and broader than they had on her way out. She nodded and smiled back to a few of them. Even Mertyl Casper was grinning like a Cheshire cat.

Shirley half-waved at her, feeling guilty for being so harsh earlier. These people were her friends. Her fellow parishioners. They weren't noting her size, they were appreciating her spirit. She sat down just as Sister Smith launched the chorus into a number called "My Mother, My Friend."

Shirley watched as confident little Sara lost her nerve. The girl sucked her thumb, stared at the ceiling, and did everything but sing. Shirley tried to get Sara to look at her so she could at least mouth the words and encourage her, but Sara refused. Shirley looked up at Samantha, but she was staring at the floor, her head almost between her knees. Shirley hoped she wasn't feeling ill.

Sean and the boys were being told to quiet down by the pastor's wife, who was sitting behind them. His back was to Shirley or she would have enlisted Sean's help in supporting Sara.

When the children began their second song, Sara looked at her mother. "Sing!" whispered Shirley. "Loud!"

Sara did just that. She sang louder and stronger than any of the other children, even the Smith kids. Maybe Shirley should have been a little embarrassed because Sara wasn't exactly on key. Instead, Shirley was proud of her daughter for giving it all she had. It would take a lot more than an enthusiastic soprano to embarrass Shirley.

"What's on your shoe, Mommy?" Sara asked when she rejoined her mother.

Shirley looked down. Immediately she felt faint. Caught on Shirley's heel was a long trail of white toilet paper. She reached down and realized it was connected. When she realized just *how* it was connected, she understood why Samantha still had her head bowed. All of the grins and winces she had encountered moments earlier suddenly made perfect sense. The tissue went from the heel of her shoe all the way up into the top of her panty hose, where she had tucked her dress—along with part of a roll of toilet paper.

Shirley wanted to die. To never have existed in the first place. How on earth was she going to remedy the problem and then make it to her car without ever encountering another human being? Especially a fellow Christian.

Shirley was cringing so low, she almost missed the littlest Miss Casper's poetry recital. She was the only child from the chorus given a solo part, and her mother was sitting tall and proud. Mertyl shot a look at Shirley that sent Shirley's self-esteem plummeting to new depths. Their eyes re-mained locked until a sudden gasp from the crowd directed their attention back to the stand.

Blonde little Miss Casper, dressed from head to toe in a floral frock, lace hat, and gloves, and patent-leather shoes, was the picture of the perfect child—a reflection of her mother's impeccable mothering ability. There she stood rocking to and fro, lifting the skirt of her dress to reveal that Mertyl had remembered every detail of her daughter's flawless outfit except one—underpants.

Mertyl Casper did not receive a Mother's Day planter. She and her daughters departed the services early. So, Mertyl is mortal after all, thought Shirley, still trying to figure out a way out of her own dilemma.

True, she *was* mortified, but she also knew that in time there would be a great deal of humor in this situation. Someday she would laugh with the rest of the family, but not today.

Today it just wasn't that funny.

Shirley did not stand when the pastor requested that all women in the congregation rise to the occasion so that Sean and the rest of the boys could pass out pansy planters wrapped in pink-and-purple foil. Shirley did, however, lift her bottom off the bench just high enough to have Sara grab the toilet paper and tug her mother's skirt free from her panty hose.

She stuffed the toilet paper as inconspicuously as possible into her purse. Then she shook her bottom and tried to free the rest of her skirt. She'd have to wait.

Samantha hurried past Shirley, stopping just long enough to say, "I'll be in the car." She was still looking at the floor and Shirley knew any humiliation she felt was nothing compared to the mortification she had caused her thirteen-year-old daughter.

A trip to the mall tomorrow should take care of that.

Shirley waited until Sean was finished. Then he brought his mother a purple-and-gold pansy in a soggy cardboard container wrapped in purple foil. He was completely unaware that his mother had walked through the whole chapel trailing clouds of not-so-white toilet paper.

"Happy Mother's Day," he said for the second time that day.

Shirley took the plant. "Thanks, sweetheart. You did a terrific job. I noticed that you got *all* of the women, not just the obvious mothers."

"Can we go yet?" asked Sara.

People were still filing out. A few had smiled and exchanged Mother's Day greetings with Shirley. A couple had come to specifically thank Shirley for the gifts they had received from her family. Shirley wasn't feeling too thoughtful or gracious at the moment. She just wanted a clear area to her backside so she could free her skirt and get out. Ten minutes passed before that discreet opportunity presented itself.

Free at last, free at last, Shirley maneuvered her way out of the chapel.

Shirley knew Samantha was waiting in the car. She did her best to hurry, but dropped the planter just before they got to the exit. Dirt and broken pansy stems spread across the carpet and all over Shirley's shoes.

She swore under her breath, then remembered they were on holy ground.

"I'm sorry, Sean. I didn't mean to drop my flower."

"That's okay, Mom," he said, kneeling to clean up the mess. "I'll get you another one, if there are any left over."

She bent over to help him.

Her water broke. Plain and simple. Not in some pristine little drizzle, but in one giant gusher.

She swore again, this time aloud.

"Something wrong, Shirley?" asked the pastor.

There she was on her hands and knees in a self-made mud puddle right in the middle of the church foyer. She started laughing. People stopped and stared. The pastor offered her his hand. But Shirley kept laughing. "Could someone please give me a ride to the hospital?" she asked between guffaws.

Eleven

Stan made it to the hospital before Shirley arrived. Someone from the church had called and informed him of his wife's dilemma. The pastor's wife had taken Samantha, Sean, and Sara home with her.

"Drugs. Drugs," were the first words out of Shirley's dry mouth. Contractions had put a sudden halt to her fit of laughter.

"I know, I know," said Stan. "I've already told them to get the epidural ready. All the paperwork is done."

She grabbed his shirt sleeve and whispered, "Bless you."

"Now I know you're in *real* pain," he teased.

The next little while was a frenzy of preparation. People she didn't know suddenly became very well acquainted with Shirley. There was no such thing as modesty in the maternity ward.

They undressed Shirley and covered her with something that reminded her of Sean's backyard teepee. They hooked her up to every kind of electric gizmo imaginable. All signs were normal.

"You're dilated to six centimeters," announced the doctor, removing his rubber gloves and tossing them into a metal garbage can with a flip-top lid.

"What does that mean?" asked Shirley, doing her best to cover herself.

"Isn't this your fourth pregnancy?"

She nodded. "How long till my baby's born, Doc?"

He smiled. "Could be within the hour or longer."

"You should run for office."

He smiled at Stan, like they shared some man-to-man secret about women. "Call me if you need me."

"If *you* need him? What about me? Remember, *I'm* the patient."

Together in the little room, Stan and Shirley did what they had done three times before.

They participated in God's greatest miracle.

A new life.

They knew their roles.

In tandem they kept vigilance at the heart monitor.

They waited together.

Stan was in charge of the cleansing breaths.

Shirley was in charge of the profanity.

Stan cheered through the contractions.

Shirley sweated.

Stan watched the Chicago Bulls battle the Knicks.

Shirley kept checking to make sure the nurse call button worked.

"I'm sorry, ma'am, but we can't give you any more medication," said the nurse for the third time that hour.

"But I still feel PAIN!"

"I'm sorry."

"No, you're not. You're not sorry at all."

Stan sighed loudly. "My wife is having a baby. Please don't pay any attention to her."

"*What?*" Shirley demanded. "Paying attention to *me* is her job, Stanley. It's yours, too!"

"Shirley, you're right," he mumbled, one eye still on the game. "I'm sorry."

The nurse returned a moment later with a paper cup and a plastic spoon, which she handed to Stan. "Ice chips can be very soothing."

"Thank you," he said, taking the cup and returning his attention to the game.

Shirley watched as Stan stuffed his own mouth with the crushed ice, crackling and popping the tiny chips, grinding them into cold water that he swallowed in gulps. The cup was empty before he turned to Shirley.

The look on her face must have told him what she was thinking. His eyebrows raised and lips stretched back in an expression of enlightenment. "Oh, sorry, babe. These were supposed to be for you, weren't they?"

Stan raced out the door to refill the cup. Then he sat and spooned ice chips into Shirley's parched mouth. She could not help thinking how bored he looked. He sat beside her and read a magazine when the basketball game ended.

"I just read the most amazing thing," he said. "Did you know that when Sigmund Freud was seventy-seven years old, he wrote in his journal, 'What do women want? What do women want?' Imagine that, I'm not the only one your sex has confused."

"Rub my feet," Shirley said. "I want you to rub my feet. Is that so difficult?"

Stan grabbed a foot.

"Not so hard," she yelled. "Not so hard!"

When it was finally over and Stan held a newborn son in his arms, Shirley apologized. "I hope I wasn't *too* awful."

Tears were in his eyes and Stan could hardly speak. "You were wonderful."

Those first few minutes of new life, an untouched miracle, were shared by mother and father in a way that no words can describe.

Love comes closest.

"What are we going to name him?" Stan asked, the baby's tiny fist in his. "Bill Cosby says if you get a name with a vowel at the end, it echoes through the house longer when you're screaming it."

"My mother will be annoyed if we go with another S name."

"How about Stanley, Jr.?" he teased.

"Taken. Remember Stanley Sean?"

"Oh, yeah. What about Scott? I've always liked Scott."

"It's my old boyfriend's name."

"Forget that one. Why didn't we start thinking of names before now?"

"Actually, I have been thinking of one for the last few days."

"Really? What is it?"

"Stephen."

Stan knew all about Stephen and understood what the name and the child meant to Shirley. "I think Stephen is a perfect name. What do you think little Stephen?" He passed the baby to Shirley. "Happy Mother's Day." Stan kissed her softly on the forehead.

Some time in the night, when the hospital was dark and quiet, and the drugs were beginning to wear off, Shirley opened her eyes and looked around. There by her bed was a sign that read: *Strong Families Are Made of Strong Individuals.* She had heard the thought before; now it made even more sense.

I'm not very strong, she thought, almost pressing the call button again, but decided against it. She didn't want to feel numb. She wanted to feel the exhilaration and exuberance of the moment.

She did push the nurse call button. "Would you please have the nursery bring me my baby?"

"But it's the middle of the night."

"I know, and I hate to be a bother, but I just want to see my son."

"I'm sure he's sleeping. You should be, too."

"I will later. Right now I need to hold my baby."

The nurse sighed, relenting. "I'll buzz the nursery. They'll have him there in just a few moments."

"Thanks."

Shirley felt like an entirely different person. Forget the fact that she had gained fifty pounds in the past nine months and that Stephen only weighed six and a half of those. It was more than the weight. Tonight she felt like a *mother*. A new mother to Stephen, yes. But she was feeling an overwhelming love and appreciation for the other children, too. She wondered what Stan would do if she phoned him in the middle of the night and asked him to bring the other children to the hospital just so she could hold them.

She was seriously contemplating it when the door opened and the nurse brought a sleeping and bundled newborn son into the room.

"Is this your first baby?" the nurse asked.

"It's my fourth."

"Your fourth! My goodness. You've got the concern and enthusiasm of a first-time mother."

"Thank you," said Shirley, reaching for her son.

The next day neither Shirley nor Stephen got to catch up on their sleep.

First, Stan brought the kids by to meet their baby brother. Sara thought the baby's head looked funny. Sean called him E.T. Samantha promised she'd baby-sit, and even change diapers free of charge.

"We'll renegotiate after the first stinky diaper," said Shirley.

Then Shirley's mother, Lena, stopped in to bring a baby quilt she'd made. "I've got everything under control at home. I'm rearranging your cupboards. Honestly, I don't know how you find anything in that place."

"Aren't you going to say anything about Stephen's

name?" asked Shirley, braced for battle. "It's another S name."

"I think Stephen's a wonderful name."

Shirley was speechless.

Half the congregation from church came by to visit and to view the new baby. After all, they felt they were somewhat responsible for Stephen's birth. The embarrassment and resentment Shirley had felt for them was gone. The pastor's wife brought by a new pansy planter.

Stan's mother and father popped in just as the church members were filing out.

"He's a cute little cuss," said Stan's father. "That boy looks just like his grandpa."

"Bald and toothless," said Stan's mother. It would have been funny if she had been joking.

"Stan just took the kids out for hamburgers," said Shirley. "I'm sure they'll want to see you."

"We didn't come by to see them anyway."

Her mother-in-law handed her an envelope. Shirley took it and felt guilty for thinking such horrid thoughts. "Thanks, Mom."

"Oh, it's not for you. It's that gift certificate Stan gave me for Mother's Day. I don't know what ever made you think I'd shop at that department store. I want you to exchange it for a gift certificate to Nordstrom's."

"I'll put that at the top of my list of things to do," Shirley said, wondering when the nurse was coming with her next dose of pain reliever.

After her in-laws were gone and the baby was nursed, Shirley closed her eyes. The door opened slightly.

"Are you accepting visitors?"

It was Rita, and she was carrying a giant stuffed koala.

"Come on in!" said Shirley. "I've been thinking about you and wondering how yesterday went. I'm sorry I messed

In My Quest for Personal Growth . . .

up the big plans. What did you do? How are Karen and little Stephen?"

Rita sat the koala on the foot of the bed. "One thing at a time. Don't worry about yesterday. You had your hands full. Karen and Dr. Memford met with Karen's husband yesterday morning. I think the family is back together. They'll need a lot of help for a while, but it looks promising."

Shirley searched Rita's expression for any doubt. There was none. "I'm so glad. Did you hear what we named the baby?"

Rita nodded her head. "I think that's sweet."

"Sit down and let's talk," said Shirley. "I'm going to be here for at least another day, or until the insurance runs out, so pour your heart out, girl. I want to know all about the mystery woman that you are."

"Not much of a mystery," replied Rita. "Just private."

Shirley sensed now was not the time to push her for the details of her life. "Okay. Then let's talk about me. Did you see my darling baby boy down in the nursery?"

"Not yet, but I'm planning a stop on my way out."

Shirley went on and on about her family. She even told Rita about her spiritual experience in church yesterday. They both laughed until Rita stood up.

"I've really got to go," she said. "But I'll see you after you get home and back into the swing of things."

"You can come back and visit me here if you'd like."

"I don't think so. This is a time for family."

Shirley suddenly realized how difficult this was for Rita. She didn't know the mystery behind her, but she knew there was a lot of pain, and some of it had to do with motherhood. Someday she would know. But for now, there was no pressure.

"Give me a hug, then," said Shirley.

Rita leaned over but then sprang back.

"What's wrong?" Shirley asked.

"You're . . . you're . . . lactating!"

Shirley looked down. On the front of her hospital gown were two big wet circles.

"Time to feed the baby again," she said, not embarrassed in the least.

Maybe she was wrong about Rita. Maybe there was no pain associated with motherhood at all. After all, real mothers didn't use terms like "giving birth" and "lactating." At least, not the mothers Shirley knew.

Stan and the kids came back later that evening.

Shirley was rocking Stephen and feeding him.

"Where do babies come from?" Sara asked.

Shirley grinned up at Stan. "Mommy's tired, honey. Ask Daddy that question later, will you?"

Sean was so thrilled to have a baby brother, he brought his favorite football as an offering.

"I don't know if that should be so close to the baby," cautioned the nurse. "It's probably covered in germs." She removed it and handed it to Sean, whose face fell as he stepped back away from his new brother.

"I'm sorry," he mouthed to his mother.

Shirley winked at Sean and smiled. "Don't worry," she mouthed back.

As soon as the nurse left the room, Shirley put the football back in the bassinet with Stephen. "He loves it," Shirley assured Sean, tousling his hair. "And we all love you."

When the family was ready to leave for the night, Shirley pulled Stan's head down and whispered something in his ear.

It made him grin. "I'll be right back," he said.

"Where are you going?" asked Sara and Sean.

"To the gift shop."

Sara immediately quizzed, "Why?"

"I wanna come, too!" said Sean.

In My Quest for Personal Growth . . .

Stan took them both and gave Shirley and Samantha a few minutes together.

"What do you think of this little guy?" Shirley asked, holding Stephen out for her to hold.

Samantha paused just long enough to confirm Shirley's suspicions.

"You're feeling a little pushed out of the nest, aren't you?"

Samantha sat on the edge of the bed, holding Stephen very gingerly. "Not really," she mused. "I guess I'm just feeling less and less like your baby."

Shirley held her close. "You'll always be my firstborn baby girl. *Always.*"

When Stan and the kids returned from the gift shop, Sara was holding a big sack. "We brought you new pajamas," she announced to Samantha.

Samantha looked a little confused.

"I thought you might like to spend the night here with me, kinda like a mother/daughter sleep-over."

"Really? Are you serious?"

"I'm serious," she replied.

That night, after a protesting Sara left with her father and brother, the nursery nurse came down and picked up Stephen. Shirley and Samantha spent the night, curled up together on the hospital bed, talking and listening to one another and the changes they were both experiencing.

When the night nurse came in to check on Shirley, she was surprised, but understanding. "The hospital rules do say that visitors are welcome *any* time."

Shirley smiled her thank-you. "You must be a mother."

"And a grandmother, too," said the nurse. "Push the call button if you need anything. I know you know how to use it."

* * *

"I'll never forget this night," was the last thing Samantha said before she fell asleep in her mother's arms.

"Neither will I, baby. Neither will I."

When Samantha was sound asleep and after Shirley had conned the nurse out of every ounce of pain medication she could, she picked up the telephone and did something she had always wanted to do, but had never dared.

"I'd like to order a dozen long-stemmed roses," Shirley announced to the only florist whose shop was still open. Then she gave the name of the hospital and her own room number.

"Sign the card: 'Happy belated Mother's Day to the greatest wife and mother a man could ever want. I love you desperately, Stan.'"

"Will that be all?" the florist asked.

Shirley paused and smiled her best drug-induced smile. "Make that *two* dozen long-stemmed red roses—your very finest. I deserve 'em!"

**DON'T MISS THESE OTHER
SHIRLEY YOU CAN DO IT! BOOKS
COMING FROM TONI SORENSON BROWN:**

**TURN THE PAGE FOR A
SNEAK PREVIEW OF**

*Validate Me Quick;
I'm Double-Parked!*
(Now Available)

FOLLOWED BY AN EXCERPT FROM

*Check the Lost and Found, My Mind Is
Missing* (Available in October) . . .

Validate Me Quick; I'm Double-Parked!

The shrill screech of the alarm shattered the dark morning silence. Shirley shot up in bed. "Who died?" she screamed into the buzzing telephone receiver.

Her husband, Stan, grunted and jabbed her in the ribs with his elbow. "It's the alarm clock."

Reality slowly came into focus.

Five A.M.

Monday morning.

The start of a new woman.

Already Shirley could feel last night's resolve waning. Five A.M. was an hour for the insane and the "in bed." Shirley placed herself comfortably under both categories. Still, she had promised herself, so Shirley rocked the phone receiver back onto the hook and slapped the snooze button on the alarm. Then she groaned and stretched, inadvertently digging Stan with her jagged big toenail.

He moaned and turned away.

I meant to get that clipped, she thought groggily.

He rolled to the edge of the bed, taking the warmth of the quilt with him. "Shirley, you're not getting up now?" Stan muttered it more to himself than to her.

Shirley sighed. "Uh, huh."

"The start of *another* new you, huh?"

"That's right, sweetheart. The start of *another* new me."

"Ouch!" he yelped suddenly. "You really do need to trim your toenails."

It was still pitch-black outside when she finally managed to drag herself from the bedroom to the adjoining master bathroom. Shirley flipped on the light switch. BIG mistake. It felt like someone had just yanked her eyeballs from their sockets, pulled them far enough to challenge their elasticity, and then let 'em flip back into place.

"So this is what early-morning euphoria is like," she mumbled, splashing cold water on her sleep-swollen face.

"What did you say?" asked Stan.

"Nothing. Go back to sleep."

"Then turn off the light so I can."

"Sorry, Stan." Shirley pushed the bathroom door closed to leave her husband in the warmth and comfort of the pre-dawn shadows.

By 6:00 A.M. the sun was still not up, but Shirley was wide-awake. She had already made it through the first three goals on her "Things to Do Today" list, more than that if you counted getting dressed and brushing her teeth. Shirley was actually feeling pretty good about herself this morning, a rather foreign feeling for this woman.

No, today wasn't her first attempt at becoming a new woman, far from it. But today was the first day of *this* effort, and this time would be different, she assured herself. This time she would tackle her goals with self-confidence and courage. This time she would turn a corner and not meet a dead end. She tried to summon up that seventh sense every woman has to reassure her of her direction, but most of Shirley's senses were still asleep.

So Shirley stretched her hands out in front of her and made a triangle between her thumbs and fingers. It was a trick she had seen Grasshopper on *Kung Fu* do many times to help him focus. "Today my mind, my body, and my spirit will be in harmony," she chanted aloud, sounding neither

Asian nor wise. "Surely, you can do this," she whispered aloud. Then she chuckled. "*Shirley*, you can do this!"

When 7:00 A.M. rolled around, the rest of the family was just stumbling from slumber. She couldn't help feeling a twinge of nervous anticipation. What would they think when her husband and children saw all that she had accomplished? There was her exercised and showered body (a major work still in progress), the makeup (lips actually lined and dark circles mostly concealed), the neatly trimmed and polished toenails and fingernails, the vacuumed carpet (with no ground-in Cheerios or even footprints crushed into the shag), and then there was the crowning masterpiece—the sparkling kitchen, the table set with real linen napkins and spot-free Sunday dishes, fresh-squeezed orange juice in frosted mugs, and healthy home-baked oat bran muffins and steaming cracked wheat cereal sweetened with honey. It was an early morning feast worthy of royalty.

Shirley stood at the bottom of the staircase anxiously awaiting the delight that was sure to register on the regal faces of her family as they raced down the stairs.

"Where's my math homework?" shouted Sean, whizzing past Shirley in a whirl.

"It's on the desk, dear, and good morning to you, too," she answered, telling herself, The boy is only seven—his behavior can be excused.

Next came Samantha. "The table looks nice. What's for breakfast?"

"Orange juice, muffins and hot cereal," Shirley announced proudly.

"Healthy stuff, huh? Sounds delicious." Samantha managed that whiny sarcasm that only a twelve-year-old can.

"Got any toast—*white* bread?"

Breakfast was even more than Shirley could have dreamed. Her family acted like royalty all right, and she felt just like a peasant woman. Custom-fit for a life of servitude.

Her husband, Stan, enjoyed his bacon, eggs and white toast. "I'm just not in the mood for cracked wheat." He had attempted an apology. Then he kissed her on the cheek. It was one of those puckered, dry, duty kisses. "Shirley, you've outdone yourself this morning."

"My feelings exactly," she agreed.

Samantha enjoyed her white toast layered in butter and honey. She did agree to sample the orange juice. "This tastes different," she whined without effort, "and it's got feathers floating in it."

"It's pulp, not feathers," Shirley corrected her, calmly digging her freshly painted nails into her own palms. Breathe deep, she told herself. After all, it was only breakfast they were attacking. If that was true, then why did Shirley feel like she was the target?

"The juice tastes different because I spent almost an hour squeezing a dozen oranges so that you would have fresh orange juice this morning," she explained between gritted teeth.

"You don't have to whine, Mom," said Samantha, gulping the juice anyway. "I just like the frozen kind better— you know, the stuff that comes in a can. It tastes better."

"I'll remember that next time."

Sean, bless his seven-year-old heart, ate three of his mother's oat bran muffins smothered in butter and fresh strawberry jam. He wasn't in the mood for cracked wheat cereal or orange juice with feathers floating in it, either. But he did think the frosted goblets were a "cool" effect—especially when Shirley failed to lunge quite fast enough to keep Sean from pouring steaming hot microwaved cocoa into his.

"I'll help you clean it up," Stan said of the shattered glass mess.

"It's okay. I can do it. Just get ready for work, or you are going to be late."

"I've got plenty of time," he said, separating himself from his wife with a wall of the morning newspaper. "Besides," he said from somewhere behind the sports section, "I thought you wanted to enjoy a leisurely breakfast together as a family this morning."

Shirley reached across the table for a piece of broken glass. A lethal weapon in the wrong hands.

"I'll help you clean up Sean's mess," volunteered Sara, who was three years old, and at the moment, aeons more mature than Shirley.

"No, honey, you could cut yourself," her mother cautioned just as blood spurted from Shirley's index finger.

By the time 10:00 A.M. rolled around, Stan was off to work. Samantha and Sean were at school. Sara was coloring creatures she had made out of the cracked wheat box. Turned out that nobody was in the mood for such a healthy, hearty cereal. Not even Shirley. But she did manage to finish off the muffins and the rest of the strawberry jam. She also downed the rest of the freshly squeezed orange juice and had to silently acknowledge the resemblance between the tiny pieces of pulp and feathers. From now on, the only competition that frozen concentrate would face for the family's morning beverage would be a diet Coke—Shirley's personal choice for that pick-me-up and get-me-started drink.

She did the obligatory once-over on the house—setting the dishwasher in motion, making sure all the toilets were flushed and the stairs were free of dangerous toys that could trip a person. Domestic duties done, Shirley then opened her laptop computer and began poking at the keyboard with her Snoopy-bandaged index finger. Suddenly she felt herself age by a decade as her body slumped and sagged.

Why does my life have to be experienced in such extremes? she wondered. This morning's high and this minute's low. It seemed like she was always tipping one end of the scale or the other. Why couldn't she just manage to enjoy the measures in between? The question was a good one and she considered it for some time. Her doctor had ruled out her self-diagnosis of a bipolar disorder. "Some people are simply more prone to mood swings," she had told Shirley. "What you need to do is learn to relax and savor life minute by minute."

For that bit of medical advice, Shirley had paid a fifty-dollar deductible and been forced to fill out a half dozen medical forms. So . . . if she didn't need Prozac or psychiatric care, what did she need? Some way to recognize and appreciate those precious measures along life's scale.

Shirley sat staring at the blank computer screen, feeling a little profound, but still mostly down. That is when she heard the voice. It was a man's voice, rich and resonant. She shook her head to clear her thoughts, then listened to be certain she wasn't going completely mad. Nope. The voice was real. Sara had turned the television on and the sound was booming from down the hallway.

"For any woman who longs to feel worthwhile, appreciated, and complete—stay tuned."

Shirley was in front of the TV in a heartbeat.

"Sounds like this is one program I can't miss," she said to Sara, adjusting the volume on the television and falling back into the comfort of the couch cushions.

"But, Mommy, I wanted to watch cartoons," protested Sara; she gripped the remote control in her tiny fist. "*Scooby-Doo* is coming on in a minute and he is going to rescue his friends from Zombie Island."

Shirley quickly, but gently, pried the remote control from her daughter's clutch. Shirley felt that she was the one in need of rescuing. "Sweetheart, you can watch *Scooby-Doo* any time. Right now, there is a program on television that Mommy really *needs* to watch. You can sit right next to me and color in your Scooby-Doo coloring book."

"But it's old."

"Next time I go to the store, I'll buy you a new one. Deal?"

"New crayons, too?"

Shirley nodded.

"Deal, then." Sara shook her mother's hand and grinned.

For the next sixty minutes, Shirley sat mesmerized while Sara continued to color. She was so engrossed in the program that Shirley didn't even notice when Sara traded her crayons for the lip-liner pencil that had been so enormously *in*effective that morning.

The infomercial man was captivating. This male Ph.D. had obviously taken his studies on women's emotions very seriously. Without ever having met her, he was able to pinpoint Shirley's problem—right there from the television screen he spoke to her insecurities and feelings of worthlessness. What Shirley was lacking in her life was VALIDATION.

How could a stranger know her so well? He was dead center. Right on. It was true that no one made Shirley feel worthwhile, appreciated, or complete. She lacked that stamp of approval that somehow made her a legitimate success.

The man combined his Ph.D. skills with powerful preaching as he had Shirley interacting with the thirteen-inch TV screen.

Could she feel the truth in his words?

"Yes!"

Did she ache to feel loved and appreciated by those she loved and appreciated?

"Oh, yeah."

Was she a broken woman?

"I'm not so sure."

Okay, if not broken, was her spirit at least bruised?

"Absolutely."

Was her goal to feel whole and happy instead of fragmented and depressed?

"You bet."
Did she want the pain to go away?
"Yes!"
Did she want it to leave right away?
"This minute."
Was she willing to pay a price to have that pain removed and replaced by joy?
"What kind of price?"
A price that was minuscule in comparison for the change it would wreak in her life.
"How minuscule?"
So minuscule, it could be divided into three easy payments that would automatically be charged to her credit card.
"Okay."

Shirley felt a tiny tug at her sleeve. "Are you okay, Mommy?"

Shirley tipped her chin. "I think so, honey."

"You're talking to the TV, Mommy. That man can't really hear you. He's not really in the box."

"Oh," sighed Shirley.

When the 1-900-VAL-DATE number flashed across the screen, Shirley had regained enough composure to recognize it for what it was. But she was desperate, and $3.95 per minute sounded like a reasonable investment at the moment.

She felt a little foolish dialing the number, and almost hung up when she heard a recorded message announce, "Stay on the line for information that is guaranteed to change your life for the better."

Shirley wanted her life to change for the better, so she stayed on the line. She felt like she had been hanging for so long now anyway, what was another minute or two?

Seven dollars and ninety cents later, she spoke to an actual person. Twenty-two minutes, or a week's worth of groceries later, Shirley had the basic formula for validation. It was simple really. Almost silly, it was so juvenile. But if it would make her feel better about herself, what did she have to lose?

The formula for validation seemed elementary enough. In a few weeks, she would be receiving a specially designed parking validation coupon in the mail. If she didn't want to wait for it to arrive, she could acquire a real parking validation or make a coupon of her own. Then she was supposed to divide it into pieces like a jigsaw puzzle. On each piece, she was supposed to write down the name of a person from whom she sought validation. When she finally felt validated by a person, she was to put the puzzle together piece by piece until it was complete. Abracadabra—Shirley, too, would be complete and validated.

"I can do this," she assured herself aloud. "Can Mommy borrow a page from your coloring book?" Shirley asked Sara.

"Will you stay in the lines this time?"

"Oh, I don't want to color it."

"What do you want it for, then?"

"I'm going to make a puzzle," she answered her daughter's query. Then she noticed that Sara had her lips, teeth, and most of her fingernails covered with Shirley's Magical Mauve lip liner. Normally, Shirley would have lost her temper at this point, but all she could do at the moment was smile and wonder what else had been going on right under her nose that Shirley was oblivious to.

Sara asked, "What kind of a puzzle?"

"I'm going to make a special puzzle so that I can feel validated."

Sara's little brow furrowed. "Will it hurt?"

Shirley smiled, licked her thumb, and began to smudge the lip liner from her daughter's face. "I sure hope not, honey. I sure hope not."

Check the Lost and Found, My Mind is Missing

Their first stop was at the end of a mile-long line to visit Santa Claus. Both Samantha and Shirley had opted to be among the first to barge through the doors of the mall's biggest department store at exactly 10 a.m. when it opened, but the whines and crying of the younger ones had won out. Mother and first-born daughter had managed to negotiate a Santa stop first in exchange for a promise of two hours of "no-whining" shopping. But by the looks of the line and the tortoise pace at which it was moving, Shirley figured the whole mall would be closed by the time they reached Santa.

"Let me go shopping around the mall while you wait in line," begged Samantha. "I'll be back by the time the kids get ready to sit on Santa's lap."

"No way am I letting you out of my sight again."

"I'm not a child, Mother."

"And I'm not having this argument."

"That's not fair."

"I'm sorry. It's not my job to be fair. I'm your mother."

Samantha snorted her displeasure.

Sara tugged at Shirley's coat. "I have to go potty."

"You'll have to wait, honey. If I take you now, we'll lose our place in line."

"I can take her," Samantha volunteered.

"No you can't. I'm not getting separated again."

* * *

Exactly fifty-four minutes later Sara was finally siting on Santa's knee.

Shirley looked *closely*. The bells jingled. The nose was big and round. The costume was red, the beard was shiny synthetic white with shades of blue, the hands were gloved and the feet donned big black leather boots. Even the belly shook like a bowl full of jelly. Still . . . she couldn't be sure, but this year's "Santa's helper" looked an awful lot like the jolly old cashier at the local Pic 'n Save store where Shirley's family shopped practically every weekend.

A *woman* Santa? Cool.

"Why don't you let Santa hold your little guy?" Santa asked, reaching for Stephen.

"Hey, Santa sounds like the lady at Pic 'n Save!" shouted Sean.

Shirley handed an unsure Stephen across the barrier and into Santa's outstretched arms. He immediately started to squirm.

"I want to have a turn," Sean announced.

"I thought you said this was stupid and you didn't want any part of it," a very bored and testy Samantha said.

Sean leaped across the chain barrier and stood by Santa's knee. "I changed my mind."

"I haven't had my turn!" Sara began crying. She could barely be heard over Stephen's terrified wails.

"Why don't you pay the ten bucks and have a Polaroid of the three of them taken?" Samantha suggested. "This is one of those moments you'll want to remember forever. It'll make a great scrapbook page." Her voice dripped sarcasm.

Before Shirley knew it, a green "elf" had taken a ten dollar bill from Shirley and was now behind a camera shouting, "Everybody look here and smile!"

Sean was trying to whisper his Christmas list in Santa's ear.

Sara was still screaming at Sean.

Stephen was dangerously close to wriggling out of Santa's grasp.

Santa looked a little desperate as he, or *she*, tried to keep the blue and white beard from completely being pulled off by the battling children.

"Everybody look here and say, 'Merry Christmas!' " the elf ordered.

The kids all looked in different directions.

The camera flashed.

The elf quickly propelled Stephen back into his mother's arms.

Sean continued his barrage of orders concerning the deluxe model of the Monster Mountain Masher.

Little Sara, however, sat immobile. The look on her face was one of frozen horror.

Shirley quickly passed Stephen into Samantha's arms and then jumped the barrier herself, knocking down the entire roped section. She didn't care.

She scooped Sara into her arms. Too late. Santa's knee was soaked and the puddle obvious to the other 999 people waiting in line.

After thirty minutes in the restroom and a brand new outfit including shoes, Sara had sufficiently recovered from her humiliation.

"Can we go shopping *now*?" Samantha wanted to know.

"Yes, Dear. I appreciate your patience."

"Why, you don't trust me to go by myself and meet you somewhere later?"

"It's not *you* I don't trust," Shirley tried to explain. "It's everyone else."

"That's healthy."

"When did you turn *thirty*?" Shirley asked, astounded at Samantha's moments of adult humor and cynicism.

"Let's go buy a Monster Mountain Masher before they're all gone," Sean whined.

"No! You guys promised Mom and I could shop without your whining for the next two hours," declared Samantha.

"But I'm hungry," Sara whined. "And my new shoes hurt my feet."

"You're in a stroller," Samantha pointed out. "I'm the one who's walking, and I'm the one who deserves new shoes."

Shirley put her hand on Samantha's shoulder and whispered. "Let's stop by the food court on the way to the department store. I'll buy the kids a burger and then we can shop."

Samantha relented, but only after Shirley promised some early Christmas presents.

The mall's food court was the only place on the planet where all the kids' cravings could be satisfied. Samantha ate Chinese, Sean had pizza and Sara wolfed down a cheeseburger and fries. Shirley ate some of everything while she fed Stephen a jar of mashed bananas she had packed.

By the time everyone had feasted on the best cuisine the mall had to offer, and Sara and Stephen were sleeping contentedly in their strollers, and when Samantha was finally appeased with enough packages, Sean was in his mother's face.

"Don't worry, Sweetheart. The human race is out numbered by Monster Mountain Mashers—two to one. They are piled to the ceiling in every toy store in the mall. I'm sure Santa's elves will have no problem finding you one for Christmas."

He wasn't about to take chances. "You understand the blue one is the most powerful one. He's the one that can crush tall buildings. He's got torpedoes on his wheels and missiles on his arms!"

Shirley ran her hand over the top of her son's buzzed hair. "Don't worry, Honey. Now help me find something for your father for Christmas."

"He wants a Harley-Davidson," said Samantha.

"A Harley has been at the top of your father's Christmas list for as long as I've known him."

"Why hasn't he gotten one?" Sean wanted to know.

Shirley grinned and teased. "Maybe your Dad just hasn't been that good of a boy."

"No way," Samantha rushed to her father's defense. "Dad's name has been on the list at the Harley dealer's forever. One of these days they are going to call and tell him his bike is in. He's going to let me ride it."

"No way, Sami!" shouted Sean. "He's going to let me ride it!"

He was trying to pick a fight, but Samantha had turned him out; she had entered that zone known as female adolescence. "Just think of all the boys that will ask me out when they know our family is a Harley family."

Shirley's mind suddenly painted a picture of black leather, greasy hair, and switchblades. "I don't want to think about it," she said. "We can't get your father a Harley-Davidson, but we can get him a new suit."

Samantha and Sean gave their mother a look of sheer disgust.

"Okay. How about a fishing pole?"

"Better," said Sean, "but it's not Harley."

"*I* want a Harley. I want a fishing pole," said Sara. "I just want one of everything. That's all I want for Christmas!"

The truth was, Shirley knew how much Stan had always wanted a genuine Harley-Davidson. No wanna-be bikes. It had to be the *real* thing. Shiny black. Brand new. Expensive as a new car. But it was all Stan had ever really asked for, and Shirley wished she could get him one. Three years ago when they had put his name on the local dealer's list, they'd been told the wait might take as long as five years.

"In five years we might be able to afford one," said Shirley.

Now, three years later, they were no closer to affording

such an extravagance, but that didn't stop Stan from dreaming about his Harley, and it didn't stop Shirley from dreaming about making her husband happy.

There wasn't much Shirley wouldn't do to make her family happy. She had once read that "the lack of money was the root of all evil." The thought made her smile.

By early afternoon all the "good stuff" had either been bought or destroyed by festive shoppers. Shirley was beat and now keenly aware what a stupid idea it was to take her children with her Christmas shopping.

Nothing she'd bought so far was on her list, nor had it been on sale. Now she had spent a good share of her Christmas budget and had nothing except a long red box to put under the tree. That "good tidings" feeling was fading fast.

"I get to tell Daddy about his fishing pole as soon as we get home!" Sara announced.

"No! I get to," Sean hadn't managed to say much all day without screaming it.

"It's supposed to be a secret," Samantha said.

"Yes, kids. Don't say a word to Daddy. He'll be so surprised," Shirley told her kids, knowing that they had never been able to keep a secret long enough to surprise anyone.

"I'm hungry," Sara announced again.

"But you just ate a whole cheeseburger and fries," said Shirley.

"Now I want vanilla ice cream with sprinkles."

"It's the middle of winter," her mother started to reason, but knew better.

They found an ice cream shop with a line of shivering people waiting for double-scoops of their favorite flavors.

Shirley was holding Stephen, assuring him that this day would really not last forever, when the girl at the counter suddenly smiled.

Shirley smiled back. It made her feel good. After all, this

Check the Lost and Found, My Mind is Missing · 115

was the season of good will toward everyone.

The girl handed Shirley a vanilla cone with chocolate sprinkles and Shirley passed it to Sara.

Shirley smiled again, again, giving the girl behind the counter a bill.

"That's sure a cute baby you've got there."

"Thanks. Keep the change," offered Shirley.

"You must be a very proud *Grandma*."

It took awhile for the comment to register. When it did, Shirley felt anything but festive: She quickly hurried her brood back into the crowds and toward the exit.

"Please, please, buy me a blue Monster Mountain Masher," begged Sean.

Shirley glared at him.

He actually shut up.

It was her best feat all day.

On the way out, they trudged through black slush across the parking lot, dragging strollers and screaming babies. By the time they reached the car everyone was wet and half-frozen, but at least they were *together*.

When they got home Stan was watching television and a blazing fire was roaring.

"I know what you're getting for Christmas!" Sara said to her father.

Shirley put her finger against her lips. "Shhhh . . ."

"Yeah, Sara," piped in Sean. "Dad's fishing pole is supposed to be a surprise, remember?"

Stan played along and pretended not to hear. He looked at Shirley and winked. "I got finished at work early, and I think I've actually caught that. "Ho, Ho, Ho spirit. What do you say we take a family excursion to the mall?"

Shirley suddenly felt very old. "Ho, Ho, Ho," was all Shirley could manage, but she said it in her best *grandmotherly* voice.

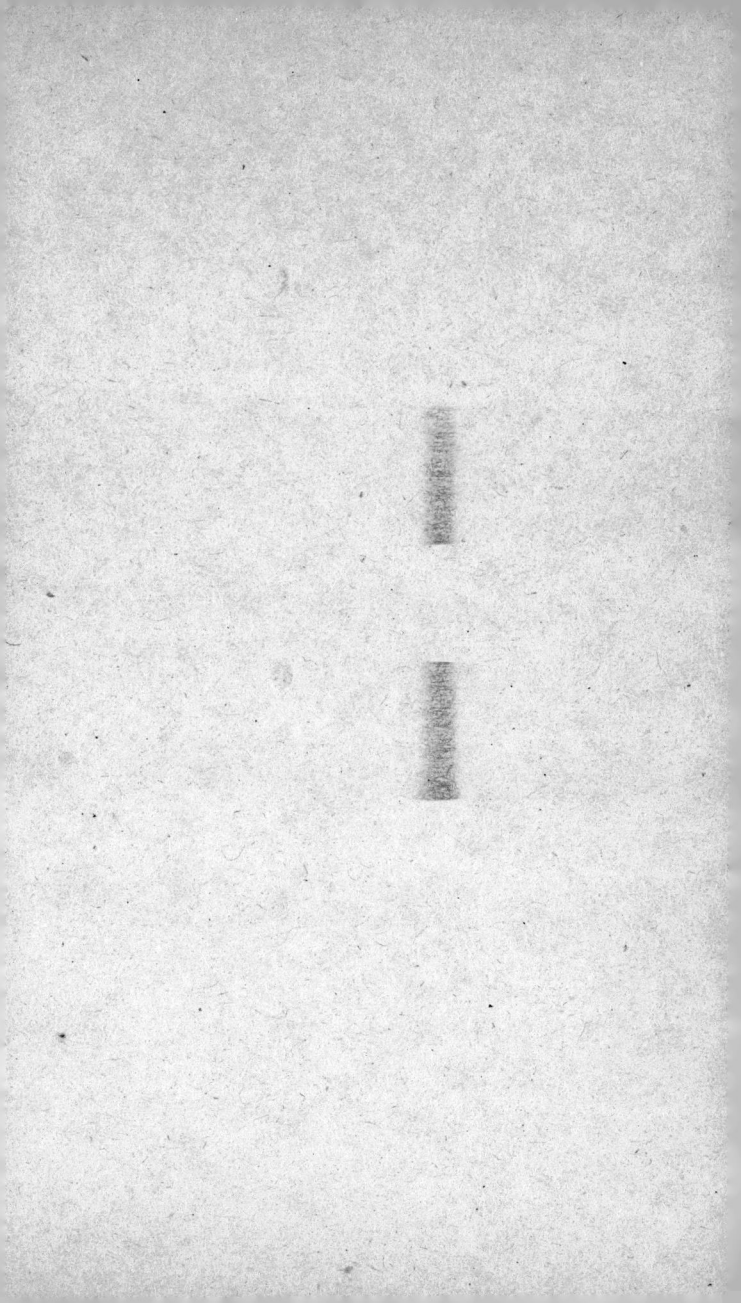